Re-disc

Praise

'His gift ... iate. **Rarely does c ... tisfying** an amalgam of plot, c ... sation and good writing.'
Punch

'Quite delightful ... with an atmosphere of quiet contentment and humour that **cannot fail to charm**.'
Daily Telegraph

'A swift-moving novel, **joyous, happy and incurably optimistic**.'
Evening Standard

'There is **such a gentle humour** in the book.'
Daily Sketch

'What counts for most in the story ... is his **mounting pleasure in vagabondage and the English scene**.'
The Times

'A paean to the beauties of the English countryside and **the lovable oddities of the English character**.'
New York Times

THE ABERDYLL ONION

COLLECTED SHORT STORIES

Victor Canning

Farrago

This edition published in 2020 by Farrago,
an imprint of Duckworth Books Ltd
1 Golden Court, Richmond, TW9 1EU, United Kingdom

www.farragobooks.com

By arrangement with the Beneficiaries of the Literary Estate of Victor Canning

Collection arranged by John Higgins

'A Matter of Time' first published in *Evening Standard*, August 1950
'A Question of Trust' first published as 'Never trust a lady'
in *Chambers's Journal*, March 1953
'Cook Wanted' first published as 'The chef who got fed up' in
This Week, April 1955
'Food for Thought' first published in *Evening Standard*, April 1951
'The Cautious Safe-Cracker' first published in *This Week*, July 1954
'Monkey Tricks' first published in *Evening News*, January 1962
'The Gorilla that Died Twice' first published in *This Week*, January 1958
'Lady in the Dark' first published in *Argosy*, October 1961
'Star Stuff' first published in *Ellery Queen's Mystery Magazine*, March 1962
'Death Wore Green' first published in *This Week*, March 1957
'The Aberdyll Onion' first published in *John Bull*, May 1959
'The White Spell' first published in *Lilliput*, May 1956
'Dialogue Behind a Curtain' first published in *Lilliput*, July 1951
'Watch Your Step' first published as 'Wet stepping stones' in *Toronto Star Weekly*,
November 1953
'Fighting Cockerel' first published in *Argosy*, November 1951
'Fill the Night with Murder' first published as 'Midnight on the lagoon' in *John Bull*,
January 1956
'Sanctuary for the General' first published in *Argosy*, August 1962
'Vintage Vendetta' first published in *Argosy*, September 1962
'The Ballerina And The Pigs' first published in *John Bull*, 12 May 1956

Ebook ISBN: 9781788422703
Print ISBN: 9781788422710

Have you read them all?

Treat yourself again to the first Victor Canning novels –

Mr Finchley Discovers His England
A middle-aged solicitor's clerk takes a holiday for the first time and meets unexpected adventure.

Polycarp's Progress
Just turned 21, an office worker spreads his wings – an exuberant, life-affirming novel of taking your chances.

Fly Away Paul
How far could you go living in another's shoes? – an action-packed comic caper and love story.

Turn to the end of this book for a full list of Victor Canning's early works, plus – on the last page – the chance to receive **further background material**.

Contents

A Matter of Time

YOU could tell it was coming. The touch, the hard-luck story … and because my own glass was full and his empty, my own suit reasonably respectable and his unreasonably shabby, I was sorry for him. Not that that stopped me from cursing myself for being a soft-hearted so-and-so who ought to be tighter with his wallet. But there it is. A man's always wondering at such times if he may not come to it himself. Twenty more years and I would have reached his sixty-odd, and a lot can happen in twenty years.

He edged along the seat a little and leaned across the table. From his waistcoat pocket he pulled a watch and laid it between us. It was a good watch, silver, and with those finely wrought gold hands that they don't put on watches these days.

"It's yours for a couple of quid. Nothing wrong with it, and honestly come by."

You could tell he was an old hand at the game by the way he ignored the preliminaries and came right to the heart of the problem at once. His voice, too, had that half-belligerent quality which some of them have, the ones who never get used to being on the wrong end of charity.

"I don't want it," I said, but because a man's money is his own and he's entitled to be a damned fool with it at times, as

I pushed the watch back to him I passed over a ten-bob note. While he was recovering from the shock I ordered a beer and a ham sandwich for him from the bar.

"I'd rather you bought the watch square," he said when the attendant had served him.

"Forget it," I said.

He took a sip of the beer to help him, but it had the opposite effect.

"I hate the sight of watches," he said suddenly, like a man remembering with a start something he'd forgotten. "They started it all."

"All what?"

"This." He flicked his hand across the front of his shabby suit and bit into his sandwich.

I had half an hour before an appointment and it was raining outside. He had me and, from the slick way he slid into his routine, I knew there was going to be no escape.

"Chris Selby was his name," the old man said. "A London theatrical agent, handled quite a few head-of-the-bill names and a great many more nearly as good. Yes, he was doing very well for himself, was Chris Selby, but he could never resist the temptation to do a little better-even if it meant going outside his own line of business."

He went into the story easily and you could tell he had had a lot of practice, which just shows that there must be plenty of soft-hearted so-and-sos in the world who are ready to part with ten bob for a story and the chance to make themselves feel a little more Christian than they really are.

The whole thing took place just after the first world war. A long time ago, but there are a lot of people who still remember it and who think the 'twenties was a pretty good period to live in. This Chris Selby, it seems, was a Prince Charming with a smile that came off and on like summer lightning, a voice like butter and eggs when he wanted something from you, and poison if you got in the way of his fifteen per cent. But on the whole few people did get in his way, and most people liked him because they didn't really know him.

He used to make five or six trips a year to Paris on business, picking up acts and vaudeville turns, trying out his smile along the Champs Elysées, and never feeling lonely in the evenings or having to count his francs to see if he had enough for another *pernod*. Twice a year he would take his car over. My friend with the watch didn't say what kind of car it was, but you can imagine—and I'll bet there was hell to pay with the garage hands if they left oily fingermarks over the wheel and dirty lumps of rag in the side pockets. He always went over Dover to Calais and back that way, and most of the Customs boys knew him and liked him because on a ten-minute acquaintance five or six times a year he was the kind of man anyone would like, and also he was generous with complimentary tickets for London shows. He never had any trouble with the Customs, and the truth was that, except for the two car trips each year, there was never any need for trouble because he never tried to get away with anything. But when the car went over—that was different. Twice a year he would bring back about five thousand watches at a time.

I know it sounds a lot, but it's surprising how many watches you can pack into a car, particularly if your twelve-gallon tank only holds two gallons of petrol and the rest watches, and the floor of the car is a false one. Of course, it means filling up with petrol pretty often on the run, but no one minds that if the gross profit on each trip touches the thousand-pound mark.

If you or I tried anything like that we'd be as nervous as kittens with a duck for a foster-mother and probably give ourselves away. But not Chris Selby. A theatrical agency is pretty good training in putting up a good front. He never felt nervous and he knew his stuff. The Customs boys seldom give a car a rummage unless they've had a tip-off or one of their investigators has picked up a lead. Of course, anyone taking a car over too often drops in for it sometime, tip-off or no tip-off. But a man going over twice a year, November and July, on legitimate business and with the high-powered personality of Chris Selby had nothing to worry about.

Now this November in question, so my friend told me, Chris set off from London feeling pretty angry. He wasn't nervous or worried about the watches he was going to bring back—he was just looking forward to seeing the man who supplied him with them in Paris—a Monsieur Audiat and his four brothers. There had been certain aspects of the batch he'd taken back in the previous July which had annoyed him and made the trip less profitable than it should have been. However, as he drove into the sheds at Dover he showed none of this. He did his act, handed out a bunch of complimentaries for a new show in town, and in a couple of hours was driving out of Calais on the Paris road.

In Paris he put up at the Hotel Balzac and that evening he went round to see his supplier. Monsieur Audiat was a modest little jeweller at the bottom of the Avenue Wagram. Monsieur Audiat—one never took any notice of the brothers who hung about in the background and were almost half-witted—was careful as well as modest. Chris Selby was his only customer for this kind of work, and he was content with a regular twice-a-year profit rather than more constant business with the risk of publicity.

The day before Chris Selby was due to go home he would leave his car overnight in the garage at the back of the shop and the half-witted Audiat brothers would have the watches all packed away in the car by the morning.

Chris Selby found Audiat and his brothers at the back of the shop and, without wasting any time on polite enquiries as to their health and with the smile turned off and the butter in his voice gone rancid, he let them have it. A thousand of the last batch of watches had been duds, most of the others hadn't come up to specification and the whole lot had been so badly packed into the car that many of them had been broken. He embroidered on this theme for about fifteen minutes, slipping in frequent references to the personalities of Audiat and his brothers, their parents and the general nature of the French as a whole. It was the kind of performance he was rather good at. In the end Audiat could have stuck a knife into his heart gladly—if it hadn't been for the fact that no Frenchman willingly destroys the source of a nice little profit—and even the half-witted brothers got the idea that the *anglais* was angry because he hadn't had watches that worked as well as looked good. However, Audiat finally explained that the batch of watches had been bought by him from Switzerland and he had had them packed unexamined in the car. When things quietened down he promised that there should be no trouble with the next batch which was arriving the following day.

But the next day the watches hadn't arrived. Nor the morning of the day after that when Selby drove his car round. Now Selby had hoped the watches would arrive that morning so they would be packed in time for him to make

Calais for the last ferry. He wanted to be in London the following day for a new show which was opening in which he had an interest. To show how he felt about things Selby examined the genealogy of the Audiat ménage again and swore that if the watches didn't come in time he'd take his business elsewhere.

Well, he spent the day clearing up a little unfinished business with a fan-and-dove dancer whom he felt he could promote professionally and privately in London, and in between whiles telephoning Audiat to see if the watches had come in. In the afternoon when he telephoned he learned that the watches had just arrived. He left the dancer to feed her doves and whipped around to Audiat. He told him exactly how he wanted the watches packed and Audiat promised that his brothers should examine them all and see there were no duds and that the car could be picked up at four in the morning, which would give Selby time to drive to Calais and make the early morning ferry. He'd be in London after lunch and make his new show in the evening. It meant Selby wouldn't get much sleep that evening, but he was used to that and he would have the cooing of the doves to rouse him if he did sleep on.

Just after four in the morning he was away, singing to himself, driving fast and practising his smile on the women at the level-crossing gates. When it was a matter of practice he didn't mind what kind of woman it was. At Calais it was a raw cold morning and he had no trouble with the douane. He saw his car aboard and then went down to the bar and had coffee laced with brandy and then dozed for an hour.

At Dover he went ashore and saw his cases through, telling the officer who was examining them not to be surprised if he shook any feathers or maize out of his pyjamas because he had just booked up a fan-and-dove dancer. Then he went over to clear his car.

The Customs officer on the car was one he knew well, a man of about his own age. He gave him the big smile, cracked the feathers-and-maize joke again and answered the usual questions. Everything went well, the smile, the joke, the easy manner and the promise of a free seat at the new show if the officer liked to write and remind him sometime.

He'd got the all-clear signal and had his hand on the car door, about to get in and drive off, when all over the place—which had been the usual pandemonium of customs clearing—there was a mad wail of sirens for a few seconds, and then everything stopped. Chris Selby didn't have to be told what it was. In those days the first world war wasn't far behind, and when the sirens went at eleven o'clock on the morning of November the eleventh everybody stopped and there was silence for two minutes. There really was silence. Even the seagulls stopped bawling their heads off. Chris Selby and the officer stood by the car like a couple of wax figures, and you could have heard a pin drop.

No one did drop a pin, but Chris and the officer heard something else. From the car, not loud enough for anyone else to hear, it's true, but loud enough to do the damage, came the gentle sound of five thousand watches ticking off, all carefully wound by the half-witted Audiat brothers who wanted to please the *anglais* by making sure that he had watches that went as well as looked good.

It was here that my friend stopped his story to finish his ham sandwich and beer. I'd had my ten bob's worth all right, I suppose, but there's always something that drives a man on to get a little more for his money, and I said:

“Now tell me that you’re Chris Selby and maybe I’ll buy the watch for a couple of quid.”

But the old boy shook his head. “Selby died years back. No, I’m the Customs officer. With his smile and his ten-minute charm he talked me into a partnership and two years later we were both caught.”

A Question of Trust

EVERYONE thought that Horace Danby was a good, honest citizen. He was about fifty years old and unmarried, and he lived with a housekeeper who worried over his health. In fact, he was usually very well and happy except for attacks of hay fever in summer. He made locks and was successful enough at his business to have two helpers. Yes, Horace Danby was good and respectable — but not completely honest. Fifteen years ago, Horace had served his first and only sentence in a prison library. He loved rare, expensive books. So he robbed a safe every year. Each year he planned carefully just what he would do, stole enough to last for twelve months, and secretly bought the books he loved through an agent.

Now, walking in the bright July sunshine, he felt sure that this year's robbery was going to be as successful as all the others. For two weeks he had been studying the house at Shotover Grange, looking at its rooms, its electric wiring, its paths and its garden. This afternoon the two servants, who remained in the Grange while the family was in London, had gone to the movies. Horace saw them go, and he felt happy in spite of a little tickle of hay fever in his nose. He came out from behind the garden wall, his tools carefully packed in a bag on his back.

There were about fifteen thousand pounds' worth of jewels in the Grange safe. If he sold them one by one, he expected to get at least five thousand, enough to make him happy for another year. There were three very interesting books coming up for sale in the autumn. Now he would get the money he wanted to buy them.

He had seen the housekeeper hang the key to the kitchen door on a hook outside. He put on a pair of gloves, took the key, and opened the door. He was always careful not to leave any fingerprints.

A small dog was lying in the kitchen. It stirred, made a noise, and moved its tail in a friendly way.

"All right, Sherry," Horace said as he passed. All you had to do to keep dogs quiet was to call them by their right names, and show them love.

The safe was in the drawing room, behind a rather poor painting. Horace wondered for a moment whether he should collect pictures instead of books. But they took up too much room. In a small house, books were better.

There was a great bowl of flowers on the table, and Horace felt his nose tickle. He gave a little sneeze and then put down his bag. He carefully arranged his tools. He had four hours before the servants returned.

The safe was not going to be hard to open. After all, he had lived with locks and safes all his life. The burglar alarm was poorly built. He went into the hall to cut its wire. He came back and sneezed loudly as the smell of the flowers came to him again. How foolish people are when they own valuable things, Horace thought. A magazine article had described this house, giving a plan of all the rooms and a picture of this room. The writer had even mentioned that the painting hid a safe!

But Horace found that the flowers were hindering him in his work. He buried his face in his handkerchief.

Then he heard a voice say from the doorway, "What is it? A cold or hay fever?"

Before he could think, Horace said, "Hay fever," and found himself sneezing again.

The voice went on: "You can cure it with a special treatment, you know, if you find out just what plant gives you the disease. I think you'd better see a doctor, if you're serious about your work. I heard you from the top of the house just now."

It was a quiet, kindly voice, but one with firmness in it. A woman was standing in the doorway, and Sherry was rubbing against her. She was young, quite pretty, and was dressed in red. She walked to the fireplace and straightened the ornaments there.

"Down, Sherry," she said. "Anyone would think I'd been away for a month!" She smiled at Horace, and went on, "However, I came back just in time, though I didn't expect to meet a burglar."

Horace had some hope because she seemed to be amused at meeting him. He might avoid trouble if he treated her the right way. He replied, "I didn't expect to meet one of the family."

She nodded. "I see what an inconvenience it is for you to meet me. What are you going to do?"

Horace said, "My first thought was to run."

"Of course, you could do that. But I would telephone the police and tell them all about you. They'd get you at once."

Horace said, "I would, of course, cut the telephone wires first and then—" he hesitated, a smile on his face, "I would make sure that you could do nothing for some time. A few hours would be enough."

She looked at him seriously. "You'd hurt me?"

Horace paused, and then said, "I think I was trying to frighten you when I said that."

"You didn't frighten me."

Horace suggested, "It would be nice if you would forget you ever saw me. Let me go."

The voice was suddenly sharp. "Why should I? You were going to rob me. If I let you go, you'll only rob someone else. Society must be protected from men like you."

Horace smiled. "I'm not a man who threatens society. I steal only from those who have a lot of money. I steal for a very good reason. And I hate the thought of prison." She laughed, and he begged, thinking that he had persuaded her, "Look, I have no right to ask you for anything, but I'm desperate. Let me go and I promise never to do this kind of thing again. I really mean it."

She was silent, watching him closely. Then she said, "You are really afraid of going to prison, aren't you?" She came over to him shaking her head. "I have always liked the wrong kind of people."

She picked up a silver box from the table and took a cigarette from it. Horace, eager to please her and seeing that she might help him, took off his gloves and gave her his cigarette lighter.

"You'll let me go?" He held the lighter towards her.

"Yes, but only if you'll do something for me."

"Anything you say."

"Before we left for London, I promised my husband to take my jewels to our bank; but I left them here in the safe.

I want to wear them to a party tonight, so I came down to get them, but…"

Horace smiled. "You've forgotten the numbers to open the safe, haven't you?"

"Yes," replied the young lady.

"Just leave it to me and you'll have them within an hour. But I'll have to break your safe."

"Don't worry about that. My husband won't be here for a month, and I'll have the safe mended by that time."

And within an hour Horace had opened the safe, given her the jewels, and gone happily away.

For two days he kept his promise to the kind young lady. On the morning of the third day, however, he thought of the books he wanted and he knew he would have to look for another safe. But he never got the chance to begin his plan. By noon a policeman had arrested him for the jewel robbery at Shotover Grange.

His fingerprints, for he had opened the safe without gloves, were all over the room, and no one believed him when he said that the wife of the owner of the house had asked him to open the safe for her. The wife herself, a gray-haired, sharp-tongued woman of sixty, said that the story was nonsense.

Horace is now the assistant librarian in the prison. He often thinks of the charming, clever young lady who was in the same profession as he was, and who tricked him. He gets very angry when anyone talks about 'honour among thieves'.

Cook Wanted

THERE is a small restaurant near the Arc de Triomphe in Paris where the cooking is the best in the world. I'm not giving its name, for the simple reason that good cooking becomes bad cooking when a proprietor tries to fit thirty tables into a room built for twelve.

I walked in one evening and sitting in a corner was Monsieur Anton Brunot, whom I hadn't seen for five years. He was looking more miserable than ever, which, as his habitual expression is that of a man faced with catastrophe, was really quite an achievement.

I sat down by him and asked him how things went.

"Badly, mon ami," he said. "I am contemplating suicide."

The patron came along at that moment and there was a period of gastronomic skirmishing while I ordered.

Anton knew more about food than perhaps any other man in the world, and when I ordered an omelette Baron de Barante, then saddle of lamb and a bottle of Musigny, I looked to him for approval. There was only misery in his eyes and he sighed like a wind tunnel. Then for himself he ordered a bowl of clear soup and some toast.

My surprise showed on my face. It was like hearing a confirmed whisky-drinker ask for malted milk.

"Mon ami, to eat no longer interests me," he explained. This from a man who, I knew, lived only for food, from a man whose father had been one of the world's five best chefs, from a man who could have been more famous than his father if he had wished.

He shook his head sadly. "Soup and toast … I live on it these days."

Anton Brunot was a large, plump man with a fluffy tonsure of almost white hair, and a pair of lachrymose eyes that fitted his glum face better than any bloodhound's. He looked about sixty but I knew he was nearer forty.

I said, "You'd better tell me about it."

"Willingly, mon ami. But first, tell me—are you looking for a job?"

"No, I'm not." I was an assistant chef at the Hôtel Balzac and was very happy there.

"A pity," he said gloomily. And then after a pause made gusty with a long sigh, he went on, "You know my father left me enough money to live on comfortably … to eat well. Where food is concerned, mon ami, I do not have to tell you that I am an artist … a genius, even."

"Then what's the trouble? Why aren't you eating?"

He told me. The war had wiped out the investments from which he drew his income, but because of his reputation as a gourmet he had become an inspector of restaurants for a famous French guide-book. He had travelled all over France, eating well and free, and deciding what rating restaurants should have in the guide-book.

But then—and I remembered that I had heard some rumour about it—he had slipped. He had begun to take bribes and to tip off proprietors when he was coming so that they could put on a show and get a higher rating. And in the end he was found out and sacked.

"My friend," he said, "after that I spent four awful months. It began to look as though I should have to take a job as a chef. Imagine," he rolled his eyes, "to cook for other people who have no respect for the true artist—*épouvantable*! But, fortunately, an idea came to me in time. I found a way whereby I could eat well again and have enough money for the modest luxuries my nature demands."

For the last three years, he explained, he had been travelling from one European capital to another, living easily. And this was how he did it.

He would pick out some house or flat where a married couple lived. He would find out their names and then he would buy a couple of theatre tickets, always in the stalls, and post them to these people with a note indicating that they were with the compliments of the management, or just anonymously from an old friend.

Now, anyone who gets free theatre tickets may spend a pleasant hour wondering why, or who the anonymous friend is—but, in the end, they will always use the tickets.

"There is no one," said Anton, "with the will to resist something for nothing. On the night, *mon ami*, I would be waiting across the road and watch the couple go out. Once they were away, I knew I was safe for three hours and in I would go. I was never immoderate, *mon ami*. Just reasonable. I would take enough money for running expenses and small luxuries and, if there was no cash about, I'd take something that could be pawned. I always sent the pawn tickets back because people are sentimental about silver cigarette-boxes and jewellery.

"And sometimes, if the mood was on me, I would go into the kitchen and cook myself a meal. But not often, *mon ami*, for most kitchens … One look and my soul would shrink! Anyway, long before the couple were back from the theatre, I would be away. It was a perfect arrangement. I travelled. I lived. I ate—and I was happy. Until last year in London."

And in London trouble had come to him.

He had been there three months and had worked his trick three times quite smoothly. Then he had picked out a couple who lived in a small mews cottage near Hanover Square. Mr. and Mrs. Richard Archer.

He shook his head dolefully. "She was elegant, *mon ami*. *Chic*. Tall, fair-haired, blue eyes like cornflowers, and a laugh that was pure silver. For her husband, he was big, thickset … just another man to pass in a crowd."

He had watched them for a week, and then he had bought his tickets and sent them along. And when the night came they went off and he went into their place.

At this point my omelette Baron de Barante came along.

"It's odd you should have ordered that," he said. "You'll see why later. But now I shall be silent while you give your attention to it." He watched me eat and his face was full of desperate envy. When I had finished, he resumed.

He had gone into the place using the key that he'd seen them put under a pot of flowers outside the door. One look at the place told him that Mr. and Mrs. Archer were easy-going, well-disposed creatures who liked comfort and the good things of life. In a desk he found an envelope with fifty pounds in it, a little more than he usually reckoned to pick up. Then, full of well-being, he had gone to have a look at the kitchen.

"*Mon ami*, it was a good kitchen. One glance told me. Your painter sees a scene and knows it is for him, that he must put it on canvas. For me this kitchen was like that. I knew I had to use it."

He had plenty of time and he had made himself an omelette Baron de Barante, a big beautiful omelette stuffed with mushrooms and shrimps, and he was just on the point of serving it when the kitchen door opened and in walked Mr. and Mrs. Archer.

"My friend, I was devastated with surprise. They weren't due back for two hours. I turned round with the pan, and Mrs. Archer gave me a smile and a polite good-evening. Mr. Archer, very bluntly, I thought, asked me to explain myself. Fortunately, Mrs. Archer came to the rescue. She pointed out that if we had the explanations first, then the omelette would be spoilt. A perfect woman …"

Mrs. Archer had got out two more plates and the three of them had sat down to it and shared a bottle of Beaujolais. "*Mon ami*, what a woman! Like a willow tree. And it was a joy to see her eat—though for my own pleasure the omelette would have been more satisfying shared between two rather than three. Over coffee I gave my explanation. I told them the truth, of course, relying on their good nature. They gave me all their sympathy and I began to think I should be allowed to leave without trouble. But I reckoned without Mr. Archer.

"I handed the money back to him and stood up, saying, 'You are two extremely understanding people. I regret any trouble I have caused you.' But it was not as easy as that."

Mr. Archer had pushed the notes back to him and had said, "Keep them, Brunot, and regard them as an advance on your wages. You're a cook in a million and when a man finds a good cook these days, he hangs on to him. You're staying with us and if you won't, I'll have to go to the police."

Anton Brunot sighed and looked miserably at the plate of soup before him. It was getting cold, and a thin film of grease had formed on the top. He pushed it away.

"*Mon ami*, I tried everything. I appealed to her, but she shook her head. I pointed out that I hated to cook regularly, particularly for other people, and that I should not give satisfaction. But she would not believe this, and rightly pointed out that an artist was an artist and could not spoil a dish if he tried. How well she understood …"

And there he was, stuck with the job. And it soon became obvious that the more cooking he did the less appetite he had himself for food. He still went on cooking brilliantly, but for himself there was no longer any joy in eating.

His employers were now living in Paris for a while, and he was over with them. He couldn't run away because they would put the police onto him and he could be easily traced. He was miserable and the only hope they had given him of release was that he should find for them a cook as good as himself. If he did that he could go without fear. He'd tried—but so far without success. How could he? He was better than his father, better than any other chef I knew.

"My friend," he finished sadly, "it's either suicide before starvation kills me, or take the risk of the police when I run away. You're sure you don't want a new position? You might just do, though you are—if I remember—a little uncertain on some sauces."

"I'm happy where I am," I said. "But, tell me—why did they come back so early from the theatre and catch you?"

"Oh, that …" he sighed. "Well, I'd sent them the tickets with the compliments of the management. But Mr. Archer didn't have to have tickets to get in. He was the man who had written the play."

Food for Thought

THE last time I'd seen Monsieur Pluvet was in the first November after the end of the war. It was outside a small hut in the hills behind Chambéry, in the Savoy. He looked glum and depressed—glum because it was snowing and he hated the cold, and depressed because even then, I guess, he was hating his job. He was in the Sûreté at Chambéry, and they had sent him out to piece together a family which a returning French soldier, in a fit of insane rage, had dismembered before cutting his own throat.

"Such an untidy man, mon ami," Pluvet had said, as we walked down to the village afterwards. "I prefer forgers. They never put you off your food."

And now here he was, four years later, the proprietor of La Reine Inconnue, a small inn well off the beaten track. His face was wreathed in smiles as he took my hand.

"*Mon ami,*" he said. "What a pleasure!"

"My friend," I said, "What a surprise! The last time I saw you, you were about to become Inspector. Now I find you an innkeeper."

"Come into the office," Pluvet said. "We will have a fine together, and I'll tell them in the kitchen to prepare us a nice duck with orange sauce and some asparagus. *Caneton à l'orange*—it is the specialty of the house. People come from a long way for it. It is good you are here today, *mon ami*, for a duck is just too much for one person, but shared between two—it is just right!"

"So, you've given up crime for the cuisine?" I said, as we sat together over our drink. "Do I smell a story in this?"

Pluvet smiled. In the old days it was quite an event if he smiled, but now it sat on his face as comfortably as a cat on a cushion. "Maybe. But deep here—" he patted his chest "—it was always what I wanted. Always I said to myself, 'Pluvet, you are a good detective, but Pluvet, you would be a better hotelier.' Watching people explain themselves, tell lies, open up their dirty little secrets—all that makes me unhappy. Watching them eat—ah, that makes me happy! Also I earn more money making them happy. That makes me happier."

"How did you find this place?" I knew Pluvet. I knew a story was there, and I knew he meant me to dig for it.

"I come here one day. I see it. I like it. I buy it. Just like that. Simple."

Little by little I got it out of him. It wasn't hard. It was just a matter of patience. It wasn't any accident which had brought him to La Reine Inconnue. He'd come out here on a case—the murder of a Colonel Thery who had lived at Chambéry.

The Colonel was rich, retired, and a widower. He was also the president of a curious little club which had been formed in Chambéry by himself and four other men. They called themselves the Chambéry Club for Eating, Walking, and the Direct Observation of Nature. It was quite a mouthful of a name, but, as Pluvet said, when a party of old fellows get together it boyish, fanciful streak often develops in them. In Chambéry itself, they were known as the Ga-Gas. Not that they were ga-ga, however. Each one had his head well screwed on, and they were all men of good position. There was the Colonel, a hell of a bore apparently when you got him on the subject of Algeria; there was a lawyer, Avocat Rochelle, a plump little man with a mind like a razor blade; a Monsieur Delambord, who was a factory-owner; André Justand, a political writer whose books were well-known in France; and a Monsieur Sainte-Verde who ran a prosperous finance company of the kind which offers to advance money without security, but never does.

"These five," said Pluvet, "they have a little ritual which goes on almost every fortnight during Spring and Summer. Every other Sunday they hire a car and drive out from Chambéry and breakfast at some little village. Already on the map they have picked out a route over the hills to some other village where there is a good inn. After breakfast they set out. Each man walks alone by his own route, and each man must do the walk within a certain time and, as he goes, he must observe nature, make little notes of the birds and flowers he sees, collect specimens, and so on. When they meet in the evening, they have a good meal, compare their notes, and elect a winner on the basis of the variety and interest of the observations and specimens collected. Childish, no? *Mais oui*—but they like it, and they do it for years. Maybe for all the years they live these five come nearest to being human and worthy people on these Sundays. Until the Sunday comes when the Colonel is murdered."

"What happened?"

"Well, it is like this. This Sunday in August they drive out for breakfast to a little village called Boisne. They have arranged to walk over the hills from there to La Reine Inconnue. They have a little discussion about what they shall eat when they get here, but this time it is not a long discussion for the specialty of this house is known and they are all for duck. But there was some argument over the wine, I believe. Then they telephone here and order the dinner and—off they go like a lot of Boy Scouts.

"It is a very hot day. And remember, they are not so young, and this time they are all a little over their time limit when they reach here. When I say all, I mean all except the Colonel. The other four—Rochelle, Sainte-Verde, Delabord, and Justand—they sit outside drinking beer and waiting for the Colonel. But the Colonel does not come. Then the proprietor who was here before me calls out that the ducklings are ready, and they go in and eat and joke a bit about the Colonel. He is getting too old to keep up with them, no?

"At 10 o'clock when their car is come for them there is still no Colonel and they are all alarmed now. Well, it is not until the next morning that the Colonel is found. A forest guard finds him up in the hills and someone has knocked his head in with a rock and robbed him. It is at this point, you understand, that I come in. I have just been made Inspector. I must make a good show. You know how it is. When you get promotion all your friends watch you, waiting for you to trip. And I have many friends."

"You never tripped in your life, Pluvet. You watch your step too carefully."

"Maybe. But what kind of a life is that, watching your boots all day long? Anyway, two days later we pick up a young gypsy lad some miles from here. He has the Colonel's watch, his ring, and some of the money he has taken from the old boy's wallet. I take him along with me. I talk to him. Maybe I talk a little roughly with him, but all I get from him is that he, is passing through the hills and comes across the body and he robs it. Robbing a dead body, you understand, is less immoral than robbing a live one. Also it is easier. This lad, he is too indignant at the fuss we make over a simple robbery to understand the mess he its And it is this, *mon ami*, which makes me think that maybe he tells the truth. So—"

"You decided to look into the movements of the other members of the club who were up in the hills?"

"*Naturellement.* They are all up there. Any of them could have done it. But why? It is always that, you understand, which is harder than the how. All of them knew which way the Colonel would walk because they all agreed on their routes beforehand. Any one of them could have slipped across and knocked his head in and then gone back to his own route.

"You know," he went on, "in a small town—if you dig deep enough—you can find a reason for any man murdering any other man. What do I find?"

"That they all have motives?"

"*Naturellement.* Take Andre Justand. He has a daughter who is in love with the Colonel's son. The son, he is in love with her—but the Colonel has refused to give his consent to the marriage. He has another and richer bride picked for his son. With the Colonel out of the way, the two can marry—and Andre Justand idolizes his daughter and would do anything for her.

"Then take Sainte-Verde. He is rich, but he is as mean as they come, and he has a wife who likes luxuries. What do I find? That when Sainte-Verde goes away from home sometimes, the Colonel was in the habit of entertaining his wife. You understand? Sainte-Verde may be mean, but he still does not like another man giving his wife a good time. You see, *mon ami*, what we find when we dig is not always pretty. Then there is Delabord. He is ambitious with his factory and the Colonel is refusing to sell him a piece of land which he wants for expansion. With the lawyer Rochelle it is even more simple. Poor Rochelle—he is in prison now. He has been embezzling his clients' money and the Colonel has found it out. They are old friends, but even so the Colonel—the soul of honour, you understand—will be forced to expose him unless he makes full restitution by a certain date. When I talked to Rochelle he admitted that the Colonel's death had come as a relief to him, although it had done him no good for his difficulties are now known. But he had expected more support from his old friend. He is a little simple, eh, to expect too much from friends?

"So, I talk to them all. I find out about them, and I have a feeling that among them is the murderer, and that the gypsy boy is just an unlucky intruder. But what am I to do? There is a great deal against the boy unless I can discover the truth."

A girl put her head round the door. "*Patron, c'est servi.*"

"Come on, my friend, let us eat."

When you're in the newspaper trade you have to learn to put your curiosity on the shelf with your hat when you eat, otherwise you develop ulcers. We ate, and it was one of the best meals I'd had for a long time. There was no question that duck was the specialty of the house. It would have been the specialty of any house. But when we got to the brie—and what a cheese, as rich and ripe as a harvest moon—I came back to the attack.

"You haven't come to the point, Pluvet. How did you find this place?"

"During my inquiries, *mon ami.* I began to like the gypsy boy. I work hard for him, and for myself because I don't want to do an injustice to an innocent man on my first case as Inspector. So I go everywhere. I go to the little inn at Boisne where the party had their breakfast. I talk with everyone. Then I walk across the hills. I walk all five routes, and you know how I hate to walk. And then I come down here and talk to everyone. That is how I find the place is for sale. But I find other things as well."

He shrugged.

"I'll bet you did."

"Finally I go back to Chambéry and I go to see Monsieur Sainte-Verde. He is surprised to see me, but he is pleasant, but not so pleasant that he offers me a drink. 'Monsieur Sainte-Verde,' I say, 'I have come to arrest you for the murder of Colonel Thery.'

" 'Very interesting,' he says. 'Perhaps you will explain a little more? Why me and not one of the other members of the club?' "

Pluvet leaned forward and filled my coffee cup. "It is a reasonable question, eh?"

"Come on, you old so-and-so," I said. "How did you know to pick on Sainte-Verde? It might have been any of the others."

"Ha, yes. You see each member of the club paid in his turn for the dinner at the end of the day's expedition. The Sunday the Colonel was murdered it was Sainte-Verde's turn. It was he, in fact, who telephoned to this inn from Boisne, ordering the dinner. He was a terribly mean man, and he knew that he was going to murder the Colonel that day. His meanness got the better of his common sense. He ordered dinner for four only—because he knew the Colonel wouldn't arrive. If he'd ordered for five they would have had to put a third duck on and, although none of it would have been eaten, he would have been charged with it. As I say, mon ami, a duck is too much for one, but just right when shared with another person."

The Cautious Safe-Cracker

HAVE you ever met the kind of man who if he goes to poke the fire has a hot coal jump out and burn his trousers? The kind who doesn't see a glass door and tries to walk through it? The kind who, when he's down to his last half-dollar, loses it through a hole in his pocket? The kind who always steps on a banana skin? Just plain unlucky.

Well, that was Artemus Wurrick. That'll show you how unlucky he was. That's his real name. He had the job here as night watchman before me. He's in the hospital at the moment.

He thought he heard a disturbance in the warehouse one night and went to see what was up. It was only a couple of courting cats but Artemus mistook them for thieves. He jumps into the shadows after them, then over a crate and breaks his leg. Sometimes of an afternoon I go round to the hospital and have a chat with him.

For a man who's had so much bad luck he's very cheerful. One day he says his luck is going to turn. Turn and bite him, I should think.

I've had a lot of bad luck, too. So, I take a kind of professional interest in Artemus. He was telling me yesterday about Alderman Staveley.

When Artemus was younger he was in and out of prison a lot, mostly for safe jobs. Long clever fingers he's got, and he knows a lot about safes. But after the Alderman Staveley business he gave it all up. It took the spirit out of him.

Alderman Staveley was a widower, about seventy, and he lived in a big country house just outside a smallish town in Kent. His wife had been a fine-looking woman and she had a very valuable collection of jewellery. Lovely stuff. But for twenty years, since her death, Alderman Staveley had just sat on it. As Artemus said, what good is jewellery if you keep it locked up? It wants to be in circulation.

He watches the place for a couple of weeks. Patient he was, and clever, too. Just bad luck was the only thing he couldn't handle. Then one night about eleven o'clock Artemus pops in through the study window. He goes over to the safe, a neat, quiet-mannered man who's just trying to get along in the world and rise in his profession.

Well, the safe gives him a certain amount of trouble but in the end he gets it open. And there are the jewels, neatly packaged in wash-leather inside a small metal box. Artemus checks them to make sure he's got them all and then he starts for the window. But he stops on the way to help himself to a drink from the study table and then, the moon coming up and lighting the room a bit, he notices something which really upsets him.

It was just the kind of thing would happen to him. Lying almost under the desk, where he'd slipped from his chair, is Alderman Staveley. And it doesn't take Artemus long to realise that he is dead. The poor old bloke must have been sitting at his desk and had a stroke or something. Anyway, he has gone. And there is a nasty cut on his face where he's hit the desk in falling.

Now, Artemus is upset about this, naturally. It's not a nice thing to happen. But he is more upset about the way things may look as far as he is concerned. If he is caught—and with his luck there is a fair chance of that—the police may argue that the old boy had come in and found him robbing the safe, and the sight had given him heart failure.

You see, normally the old boy didn't open his safe and check his jewels from one month's end to another. Artemus has been banking on this to give him plenty of time to cover his tracks. But now, Artemus argues, the first thing the police would do when the Alderman's death was discovered would be to examine the safe. Artemus doesn't quite know how—if he is caught—he will stand in law. But manslaughter, he thinks, may be the least he'll get.

Out he goes from the house and heads back for the town and Artemus is a very worried man. But like I said, he's clever and his brain is working fast and he soon knows what he must do. He must hide the jewels and give himself a reasonable alibi.

It's at this moment that Artemus comes to some fork roads just outside the grounds of the house, and there in the middle of the triangular patch of grass where the roads meet is an old well. Artemus knows the district like the back of his hand and he knows this well. It's a broken-down affair with a little wall round it, about twenty feet deep, and with never more than about two feet of water in the bottom. Just an old rainwater well that no one ever used.

So Artemus drops the box with the jewels into it. The heavy box sinks, and Artemus makes for the town. When things have blown over he knows that he can come back and get the box.

He feels a bit happier now, but there is still a lot to do. The safest place for him, Artemus works out, is to be in the hands of the police. What he wants is to be caught doing some smaller job in the town. If the police nab him doing that they will never think he's had anything to do with a jewel robbery at Alderman Staveley's the same night. It just isn't reasonable.

In the main street, Artemus picks a tobacconist's shop about two doors down from the police station. The tobacconist lives over the shop.

When Artemus came to this part of his story, he really sounded grieved, and I don't blame him.

"Know what I did?" he said. "I chucked a brick right through the glass of the door. Hell of a noise it was, just after midnight. And not a soul took any damned notice. So I put my hand in, unlocked the door and banged it open. There's a dog lying by the counter. Big as a horse almost and it just wags its tail at me friendly-like."

Artemus does everything. He takes the money from the till letting the bell ring loudly, and while he is doing it a policeman walks by outside and notices nothing. Only professional decency keeps Artemus from shouting to him.

And so it goes on with Artemus getting more and more worried. He wants to be caught and no one is taking any notice of him. He told me, "I filled my pocket with the till money. I fixed myself up with cigars and then I went through the back to the kitchen and got myself a cold supper and made a pot of tea. I couldn't find the tea caddy, at first. And I swear to you that if I'd called up the stairs to the tobacconist to tell me where it was he wouldn't have woke up. That was the kind of luck I was having. Always have had, for that matter."

He has his supper and he bangs about in the kitchen and he feeds a few scraps to the friendly dog and then, short of going up to the tobacconist and waking him, which again professional ethics wouldn't let him do, he knows he has done everything. So he decides he had better leave the place and find some other shop to ransack. There is a grocer's shop next door to the police station.

So Arternus starts to leave the tobacconist. But when he is about to go out of the door his luck turns. Not the way he wanted it, of course. But it does the trick for him. He has one foot over the threshold when the friendly dog changes its mind. It goes for Artemus like a lion.

It bites his arm and his leg, tears his clothes to ribbons and there is Artemus lying on the pavement screaming his head off. He showed me some of the scars. He was in the prison hospital for two months and he's walked with a slight limp ever since.

Oh, yes, the police got him. The noise he made woke practically the whole town.

"Six months," said Artemus, "was what I thought I should get. I knew the magistrates in the district were pretty lenient. But it didn't turn out that way. You see Alderman Staveley was chairman of the bench and the old boy—I've got to say this for him—was usually quite decent. But with him being dead they had a new chairman, and he was a real martinet. I got eighteen months. Still, on the whole I didn't mind. When I came out, the jewels would be waiting. And the main thing, anyway, was that nobody ever connected me with the jewel robbery at Staveley's place."

Artemus got some time off his sentence for good conduct and, while he was in, made up his mind that once he was out and had cashed the jewels he was going to give up the profession, emigrate and settle down somewhere comfortably.

Well, he comes out. But like I said he was clever. He doesn't go dashing back for his jewels right away. He waits a month and he grows a moustache and eventually he goes back to the place.

He tests himself by going into the tobacconist's he'd robbed and buying some cigarettes. The tobacconist doesn't recognise him. The dog never even gives him a second sniff.

So that night, a beautiful night it was, Artemus strolls out towards Alderman Staveley's place. It's about eleven o'clock. There's no one about, and he isn't even worried about having to climb down the well and grope in two feet of water for the jewel box, though he knows with his luck that it will certainly give him a streaming head cold for weeks.

"Yes," said Artemus, "I was feeling good. It had been a long time, but worth waiting for. The jewels the old Alderman had sat on for so long were going to go back into circulation. But what do you think? I turns the corner and goes up to the grass patch in the fork roads and there is the Alderman, as large as life, larger in fact, and still sitting on his jewels."

There was a bit of a tear in the corner of Artemus' eye as he told me this. He took one of my cigarettes and, as he struck a match to light it, the burning match head broke off and scorched a hole in his hospital sheet.

Yes, plumb over the place where the well had been was a statue of the Alderman, sitting in a chair; a statue erected by the citizens of the town in gratitude for his many services and philanthropies.

And to give it a good foundation, Artemus learned later, they'd just poured concrete into the well. A little fortune, buried securely under tons of concrete, and the Alderman sitting pretty on top.

Monkey Tricks

ARCHIE had a way with animals, dogs chiefly. Archie only had to say a few words, cluck his tongue. and the fiercest Alsatian would come and lick his hand.

It went for other animals, too. But with dogs it was the greatest advantage—for Archie was a cat burglar, and most dogs have the same feelings about cat burglars as they have about cats. Archie never had any trouble. Until this particular night—and then it wasn't with a dog.

He had marked down a house near Regent's Park and about half-past nine—a good time because people were then out at the cinema or the theatre—he went up a drainpipe at the back of the house, along a ledge and into a bedroom. He switched the light on and took his time. It was a woman's room, done in real style, but there didn't seem to be a thing in it for Archie until he spotted a small jewel box, a long, thin thing left out on a small bedside table. There was a diamond choker in it that almost knocked his eyes out. Archie decided to call it a night.

He switched off the light and went out of the window. But half-way along the ledge, maybe because he was thinking of the good price he'd get for the choker and, not watching his feet, he slipped.

He dropped twenty feet, hit the top of a large wire netting enclosure, went clean through the netting—which broke his fall somewhat—and landed on his back, winded and half stunned.

He lay there for a moment or two getting his breath back and, as he did so, something shuffled across to him. gave him a smacking kiss on the side of the face, took the jewel-case from his hand and then jumped up the side of the enclosure and swung through the hole in the netting at the top. Archie struggled to his feet and looking up saw that it was a large chimpanzee.

Now Archie was no fool. His fall hadn't made much noise. A few yards away, beyond the wall of the back garden, was the lighted street. He just wanted the jewel case back and to be away.

He clucked his tongue and made soft animal talk to the chimp, and the chimp nodded its head vigorously, pouted its thick lips and tapped the top of its head with the case. Then it walked along the top of the cage and dropped down into the garden. With an inviting look back at Archie it shambled towards the wall.

Archie went after it. The chimp swung to the top of the wall, did a happy jig as it saw its friend and deliverer from captivity following, and then jumped to the street outside. Archie followed. Dropping on the other side of the wall he saw that the street was fairly empty, but at the far corner by a lamp-post under a tree there was a fruit barrow with a man running around it.

Archie sprinted for the corner just in time to see the chimp go up the tree with a bunch of bananas in one hand and the jewel case in its mouth. On the first branch the chimp transferred the case to one of its feet and, pouting and nodding down at Archie, began to tackle the bananas.

The barrow boy said, "That 'ere little perisher yourn?"

Archie thought quickly. All he wanted was the jewel case and no publicity. "Yes, it's mine. Escaped from my back yard. I'm boarding it for a circus."

"Ten bob," said the barrow boy. "He's 'elped 'isself to the best bunch of bananas on the deck. And there's the shock to me nervous system."

Archie obediently handed over ten shillings. Then, standing beneath the tree he began to talk soft animal talk to the chimp. The chimp threw down a handful of banana skins and then, in gratitude no doubt, a whole banana for Archie.

" 'Appy little perisher, ain't he?" said the barrow boy. "You want him, mate, you got to go up arter 'im."

"Not me," said Archie. Archie understood animals. "You watch." He began to walk away from the tree. When he had gone fifty yards, the chimp came down and lolloped swiftly after him.

Archie turned and waited. The chimp came up to him and stood there, rubbing the top of its head.

"Come on," said Archie and he held out his hand. The chimp took it and they walked off down the street and around the far corner and along to a dark side alley where Archie had parked his car. On the way Archie was debating the possibility of persuading the chimp to give up the jewel case. But he knew the chimp would do this only in its own good time. He had no intention of brawling with it in the street and having a policeman down his neck. He opened the door of the car and the chimp, after a preliminary dance of joy, jumped in alongside the driver's seat.

"Just behave yourself and let me do the driving," said Archie. The chimp nodded and began to bang the jewel case on the windscreen. Archie winced a little and then drove off.

Not for all, the tea. in China would Archie have gone to his own rooms. He headed for the flat of his girl friend Nancy. Nancy was a girl whose advice he valued, and he wanted advice at the moment.

The chimp enjoyed the ride. On the way he whipped Archie's fountain-pen from his breast pocket, bit it neatly in half, didn't enjoy the taste, and threw the pieces through the window. Archie swore but kept his hands on the wheel. A torch from the dash pocket went next and then fifty cigarettes and a bottle of Dior perfume which Archie had meant as a present for Nancy. Obviously cars went to the chimp's head. Archie was glad when the ride came to an end.

Hand in hand they went up to Nancy's flat. Nancy lying on a settee and eating chocolates, took one look at them as they entered and said, "You can take that mucky, little beast right out of here."

Before Archie could answer the chimp dropped the jewel case on the floor, grabbed the box of chocolates from Nancy and went up the curtains.

It swung along the rod and came to rest on top of a corner cupboard. In the process a picture crashed from the wall, the curtain was ripped and a prize piece of Dresden china was knocked from the cupboard.

Nancy jumped up with a scream. The chimp selected a chocolate and showered the rest down on to Archie. It then leaped down from the cupboard to the table and on to the sideboard and, before Archie could move, had got a bottle of gin uncorked and was pouring the contents solemnly on the floor. As Nancy shouted and Archie swore it pouted its lips in a loving kiss towards them. Archie went over, took the bottle away, and held its hand.

"What am I to do with it?" he asked the angry Nancy, and he went on to explain the position.

Nancy picked up the jewel case from the floor and put it in the table drawer. "Look, stupid—we've got the diamonds—but there's only one sensible way of getting rid of that animal."

She came over to the chimp and began to examine the collar round its neck. The chimp put its arms around her and nuzzled against her cheek. Archie, despite his frustration at this moment, didn't blame the chimp. Nancy had that effect on him, too.

"You know what?" asked Nancy. "This thing belongs to Robert and Helen Safari—the famous explorers and TV personalities. That s where you did a job tonight. All you've got to do is take it back and hand it over. Say you found it wandering in the street. Best alibi in the world for you to go back there. You'll get a reward as well as the sparklers. Now get going before he wrecks this place completely." The chimp grabbed at a bottle of whisky but Nancy whipped it away just in time.

"By the time I get back he'll have wrecked my car."

"The sparklers will more than pay for any damage it does. Get going."

So Archie went off with the chimp back to his car. Fifteen minutes later, and with the radio of his car ruined because the chimp had jerked all the control knobs out, Archie was shown into Mrs. Safari's sitting-room.

The famous Helen Safari, beautiful in a theatre gown, held out her arms and the chimp bounded into them. covering her face with kisses.

"Oh, where did you find him? Oh, you good man to bring him back. When I got back from the theatre I went to say goodnight to him and he had broken out. He's done it before and he usually comes into the house and plays hell … Don't you, darling?" She kissed the chimp.

"I found him in thy street and saw the address on his collar." said Archie. "He's a valuable animal. I'd say."

"Oh, he is, and full of such high spirits."

At that moment the chimp put its paw into its mouth and pulled out something which made Archie's eyes goggle It was the diamond choker. At some time in its travels the chimp must have opened the case and pouched the diamonds.

"Oh, naughty boy—you have been in Mummy's bedroom then." Helen Safari kissed the top pf the chimp's head—which wasn't exactly what Archie would have liked to have done at that moment.

A few moments later Archie was out in the street, his thoughts grim at the prospect of facing Nancy. The chimp had done quids worth of damage to his car and the flat, and all he had got on the credit side was an autographed copy of Helen Safari's latest book—*A Chimpanzee in My Drawing Room.*

The Gorilla that Died Twice

THE man behind the small ship's bar said "I'm English, all right. But you don't catch me going back to England. Not never."

He gave a faint little smile, poured some brandy into my coffee and a larger helping into his own. "Some people, the wrong kind of people, have long memories. I've kicked around and I've kicked around. Kicks we can all take. The bruise heals. But there ain't no cure for a knife in the back or a bash over the head with a piece of lead piping. "

He sipped at his coffee and I waited for him to go on. At three o'clock in the morning and after a few brandies a man will usually go on.

The ship's bar was full of people, but except for the two of us they were all huddled in chairs or on the floor in uneasy sleep. Outside in the lounge I could see a couple of nuns bent forward with their heads down on the cabin table. Beyond them other forms were stretched out on chairs and sofas. These Spanish steamers running between ports in the Canary Islands have about four cabins and carry about two hundred passengers. The trips are mostly night trips and the few cabins always go to women and children.

"Married out here," the barman said. "Wife and two nice kids in Tenerife. Happy, too. That's the way I want it. That's why I'm not keen on going back to England. Not that I could have known what was going to happen to Sam French, though. How could I have known?"

"Known what?"

"About the gorilla and Sam French. You fond of animals? Next to kids, I'm crazy about them. I remember an old bull terrier I had—"

"Tell me about the gorilla", I said. We had a lot of night still to pass and I didn't feel like sleep.

He blinked his eyes rapidly and I could see that want of sleep and too much brandy had thawed him.

"Sam French," he said, "was the biggest, strongest, meanest, most black-souled man that ever did a stretch in Dartmoor. Know Dartmoor prison? No one ever got out and stayed out—except Sam French. He never went back."

He was started, a mild-faced, bald-headed little man behind the bar of a Spanish steamer, and there was no stopping him.

Sam French was in Dartmoor for a fifteen-year stretch. With a friend, Art Angel, he had held up a bank messenger, and they had got away with quite a few thousand pounds. The bank messenger had been killed. He wasn't the first man Sam French had killed. But somehow Sam only got fifteen years, and Art Angel, on a technicality, got nothing, not even a share of the money, because Sam had hidden it and wouldn't tell Art where it was. Wouldn't tell, that was, unless Art got him out of Dartmoor.

"Art was clever," said the barman. He smiled to himself as though he was enjoying some faint but pleasant memory. "Nothing much to look at, only half Sam's size, but he had the brains. And he went to work on an escape plan. You know that prison, slap in the middle of a barren moor. The moment a man's away everything closes down—all roads blocked and a devil of a chance has a man got of getting off the moor. But Sam did, thanks to Art. And to Bill. Mustn't forget Bill Hudson. No, that wouldn't do." He grinned and gave me a tipsy wink.

The ship rolled a little and a man by the door began to snore gently.

Art, it seemed, had this friend, Bill Hudson, who ran a small menagerie in a travelling circus. Each autumn the circus made a tour of the West Country ending up in Plymouth and then heading back across Dartmoor to begin another circuit in Wales. Well, with Bill Hudson Art worked out a plan for Sam French's escape.

"It was really very simple," said the barman. "All the best plans are. Bill Hudson, the menagerie man, was a bit against it at first. He was a great worrier. No wonder he was bald before he was thirty. But a nice fellow, really, though completely under Art's thumb, so in the end he agreed. In his menagerie Bill had a hulking great brute of a gorilla. Come to think of it, the only difference between Sam French and the gorilla was that Sam French wasn't covered all over with hair. Vicious, bad-tempered, and both killers. Why, at Plymouth the gorilla had badly mauled a child and killed a dog that got too close to its cage."

He went on, "Anyway, the idea was that after the show at Plymouth, when they took the road across Dartmoor, Bill and Art were to poison the gorilla. They would stop on the road—you know, pretend a breakdown—and bury the gorilla at night in some quiet field or wood. Nobody would know the gorilla was gone because the trailer cage always travelled shuttered up.

"They got it planned that with the rest of the circus they would be crossing near the prison the next day when Sam French would be working with an outside party—farm work or breaking stones in the quarry. All Sam had to do was break away, reach the circus, get into the cage and take the gorilla's place."

"But the moment the shutters came down or the police searched the circus, they would spot him," I said.

The barman chuckled. "Not a chance. Art had been over to Germany and got a taxi-thingummy."

"Taxidermist."

"That's right. He'd got a gorilla skin made up, head and everything, that Sam could slip on. No one could tell the difference, not even the menagerie boys who fed and watered the animals, and certainly no policeman would go poking too closely in that cage. Believe me, that gorilla had got no reputation for nice manners. It was a lovely idea. And it worked. It worked like a dream. All Sam had to do was to play the part of a gorilla for a few days. You think we ought to have another drink?"

We did, and this time we had the brandy without the coffee, and he swayed a little behind the bar. But it might have been from the roll of the ship because the wind was working up a swell.

"Yes, Sam French got away. The plan with all its timings was passed to him in prison and, when the day came, luck helped him because there was a heavy afternoon drizzle making visibility bad. He broke away from the party as they were marching back to prison and half an hour later he had reached the circus as it came across the moor making for Bristol. He was in the gorilla cage without anyone but Art Angel and Bill Hudson knowing about it.

"Course the police stopped the circus and searched it, but they took the gorilla for granted. They didn't see Art Angel either. After burying the real gorilla he'd gone back to Plymouth to get out of the way. I told you Art was clever. He didn't want to be seen within fifty miles of the circus until it was well away from Dartmoor. So he waited while the circus made its way to Wales.

"The circus did a three-night stand in Bristol and, believe it or not, Sam went on exhibition as a gorilla." The barman chuckled. "Bill was worried about it, of course. Always inclined to worry, was Bill. He needn't have, though—nobody knew the difference. Anyway, some days later Art set out for Wales where the circus was. He could hardly wait to have a word with Sam about the money."

The barman stopped there and began to wash some glasses in the sink under the bar. He seemed to have forgotten me, so I said, "Is that all?"

"All? Well, I suppose it is as far as Sam French was concerned. Not his real name, of course. Got to be careful about names and people with long memories."

"But what happened? About the money and so on?"

"Nothing. Art didn't get a word out of Sam French, not a word."

"Why not?"

"Well, he and Bill went along to the cage just after midnight, opened the little door and went in. There was Sam French curled up in the straw in one corner with a bunch of bananas at his side and half a bucket of drinking water. Drank a lot of water, he did—being in that skin made him so hot. Yes, Sam was there all right, but he couldn't tell Art anything. He was dead."

The barman shook his head. "Yes, dead as a doornail he was. Art and Bill got to the bottom of it in the end, of course. And so did the police, and it all came out in the press. Sam had been poisoned by one of the menagerie boys who brought round food and water for the animals. Kind-hearted sort of kid, he was, fond of animals, particularly dogs, and he had a soft spot for children too. The gorilla had mauled and killed his bull terrier and half killed a child who'd come too near the cage at Plymouth, so this lad decided to do the gorilla in and slip away. And he did, right away. Never heard of again. Put poison in the gorilla's drinking water."

I saw the barman two days later, walking up the main street of Santa Cruz in Tenerife. It must have been his day off. He had his wife and two nice children with him, and trotting behind them was a white bull terrier. I gave him a smile and a nod, but he looked right through me.

Lady in the Dark

FROM the bus shelter on the far side of the road he saw the only lighted window of the third floor flat go black. His eyes came down to the swing doors of the entrance to the building. The light came warmly through the entrance to the cold of the thickening dusk.

After a little while a girl passed through the doors and paused at the top of the steps, pulling the thin fur collar of her coat close up about her neck. He watched her come down the steps, turn to the left, and disappear along the darkening road. He had plenty of time. She would be gone for two hours, he knew. He knew so many things. It wasn't difficult to find out all you wanted to know—so long as you were patient and intelligent.

He crossed the road, feeling the wet autumn leaves slip a little under his feet. He passed the main entrance, turned the corner of the building, and went through a side door. Service stairs, guarded with an iron rail, stretched bleakly upwards, grey and institutional under naked bulbs. He climbed to the third floor and with his gloved hands pushed open a small door on the landing. He came out into a chandelier-lit stretch of thickly carpeted corridor.

Away on his right he heard the whine of the lift coming down from the higher floors. He waited until it had passed and then went along to the front door at the far end of the corridor. A brilliantly polished brass plate read Mrs Walter Courtenay.

He turned the handle and went in. It was never locked when the maid went out. The old lady didn't like to be locked in. If she rang for the porter she didn't want to have to come and fiddle with a key. Not at her age, not the way she was. He stood just by the door but inside him was a confident feeling of familiarity with the flat. Four months ago the identical flat on the floor below had been vacant. He had looked it over.

He turned and reached up above the door and with a pair of pliers nipped the thin wire of the bell. He hated uniformity of design, but it had its advantages. In all the flats the bell wires ran the same course.

He crossed the little hallway to the door of the sitting room, a room which he knew overlooked the street from which he had watched the flat. But it was not in this room that the light had gone out. That had been in the maid's room to the left. He went in boldly, closing the door firmly behind him.

At once a voice said, "Who is that?" It was the first time he had heard her voice and it was much as he had expected, thin, fragile—like herself, for she must be over eighty—yet with a touch of authority, that pervading tone which he hated, because he would never have it, of culture, wealth, and of easy times and rich places … in fact, the whole damned snobbish aristocratic who-are-you-my-man note.

He said, "Never mind who I am. And don't trouble yourself to start ringing bells. I've cut the wires. And don't get alarmed. I'm not going to hurt you."

He went forward and sat down on a chair by the big flat desk. There was a certain amount of light in the room from the street lamps and he could just see her sitting in a stiff chair on the other side of the desk. He could make out the white hair, the erect back, the dull gleam of a cameo brooch at the throat of her dress, and could smell a faintish lavender scent. She had her hands up a little and he saw that she had been knitting when he entered the room.

She said, "It's a most extraordinary introduction. What do you want?"

"I want the key to your safe."

"And a most impertinent demand."

He stirred in his chair, feeling the anger in him rise. The thing was now so nearly over and done with that he was impatient. You got impatient if you lived for a thing for years, got easily angry in front of this kind of talk.

"I said I wouldn't hurt you. I won't. I just want your key. Your maid's out for two hours. You can't ring for the porter. There's nothing you can do."

She moved forward a little in her chair and put her knitting down on the desk. But he noticed, even in the gloom, that one hand still played nervously with a long knitting needle. She might seem in control of herself, but she was nervous all right. That suited him.

"I understand. And when you have the key, I presume you will take my jewels?"

"That's right." He laughed. "They add up to a good life for me from now on."

"So you have not had a good life—as you call it—up to now?"

"I'll say I haven't."

"I see … you are that kind of young man."

"How do you know I'm a young man?"

She shook her head gently and her hand tapped nervously on the desk blotter. "I have been blind for twenty years, but that only makes it easier to tell some things. You have a young man's voice. You carry a great load of resentment with you, too. You feel that you have been denied privileges, but you are a fool to imagine that this is the way to right such things."

"Just give me the key. You can tell the police later that your jewels were taken by an under-privileged young man who never went to a decent school. It'll be a great help to them in picking me out from about ten million others."

He pulled a case from his pocket and lit himself a cigarette. For a moment the flare of his lighter showed up the old lady's face, a small, delicate, withered face, like some pale fruit. "I want that key. If you won't give it to me, I shall take it from the chain you wear about your neck."

"Listen to me, young man—" momentarily anger livened the frail voice at the suggestion of such an assault, and she tapped with her knitting needle at the desk, calling him to order "—I have no intention of giving you the key. What is more, I advise you to leave at once. I can give the police a much better description of you than you imagine. But if you go now I will forget this unpleasant interlude."

"You don't frighten me, and I've wasted enough time. The key!"

"Once more, for your own good, young man, listen to me. Go away at once. Go away and work for the things you want. Do you think because I am blind that 1 am helpless? Of course I'm not! I know already a great deal about you which would help the police if you took my jewels. A young man, about five feet ten—voices come from different levels, you know—and wearing a bowler hat, but probably not carrying an umbrella because you wear a raincoat. I can hear it crackle as you move. And I am glad to know that you had the courtesy to take your hat off when you came into this room. Also the grace to be nervous—for you are constantly tapping at the top of your bowler hat as you hold it on your knee. And from the tap I am fairly sure that you are wearing gloves. Also you smoke—without my permission—some kind of American cigarette. It is certainly not English."

He laughed contemptuously. "It's still a description which would fit thousands and thousands in this country. Why should you worry about your jewels? You've got plenty of money. But I haven't. I'm going to have a taste of the things you've enjoyed all your life."

The old lady was silent for a moment, and then she said quietly. "You would take my jewels because they mean money. I never regard them that way. To me, they are memories. They all mean something in my life. If you think I am handing you the key to my safe so that you can walk out of here with my memories you are mistaken."

He stood up, anger spurting in him now. "You're a stupid old woman. What do I care about your memories, about your past? Each jewel a memory!" He laughed harshly. "Well, I'll tell you what I think of your memories. Your husband's photograph in the gold and emerald locket. The lock of hair from your child in the back of the diamond brooch—memories are worth nothing to me. Jewels mean money. Just that for me."

As he moved to go round the desk, her head came up from the position of relapse into which it had sunk at his outburst. Her hands shook with a rapid, indignant movement, and she said vigorously, "Don't dare to come near me! Don't dare, you monster!"

"Then give me the key!"

"You fool—you stupid fool! Go away!"

But he did not go away. He moved slowly round the desk and stood at her side. If it had to be this way, it had to be. He had come too far, dreamt too long of this, to back away now. Even so, there was something in him which hesitated at the thought of using force on such an old woman.

He paused at the side of the desk, seeing her pale oval face dimly through the gloom of the room as she turned in her seat to face him, and he said, "Come on, the key. You've got no choice." He nipped out his cigarette with gloved fingers and put the stub in his pocket carefully.

But she shook her head. "I will do nothing to help you. Nothing."

He lost his temper then. He stepped towards her, reached out, and grabbed her by the shoulder, feeling the frailness of her body under his hands. She jabbed at his hand with her knitting needle and he caught at her wrists with one hand and held her. Swearing to himself as she squirmed and wriggled, his free hand went to her neck, searching for the chain. He jerked it free, tossed it into the palm of his hand and felt the shape of the safe key.

It was then that he heard her groan and felt her body slump back from him, pulling at the hand with which he held her wrists. She collapsed limply into her chair and he let her wrists go. She made no move.

He stood there for a moment, undecided. She was an old lady. He didn't want it to be true. He had never meant it this way. It couldn't be true. In a few moments she would recover. He went over to the wall and found the picture that covered the safe. It couldn't be true. She would have come round by the time he had collected what he wanted. Nothing could be allowed to stop him now. Not after all the weeks of patient work … listening to her maid talking to her boyfriend in the saloon bar three miles from here where she went on her night off … his back to them, his ears wide. The safe behind the picture, the chain with the key about her neck. All the work and patience.

He piled the jewel cases into the pockets of his raincoat and when the safe was empty he went back to the old lady. He put his hand on her heart, felt her pulse. It was true. It was true! She was gone. Shock. Excitement.

Well, what did it matter? He had what he wanted. Perhaps it was just as well it was like this—she couldn't even tell the police the few pathetic scraps she had gleaned about him.

AT TEN O'CLOCK the next morning Detective Inspector Burrows walked into the small but high-class jeweller's shop of Albert Munster and Son to keep an appointment he had made earlier over the telephone with the manager.

Alone with the manager in his office, Burrows said, "I believe a Mrs Walter Courtenay was a customer of yours?"

"That is so. Once every two years her jewellery came here to be cleaned."

"How many people in this shop would handle the stuff?"

"There are only three of us here—myself, my assistant, and the man we have in the workshop who does the actual cleaning."

Burrows looked across at the manager. He was very short, fat, and well over sixty. He said, "I don't think you fit the bill."

"What bill, Inspector?"

"Of the person who last night robbed Mrs Courtenay of her jewels. She was found dead by her maid."

"Dead! How terrible. Poor Mrs Courtenay. But—but, Inspector, what has this to do with us?"

"You'll see." Burrows fished a piece of paper from his pocket. "What I want is a young man, not a public school type, height about five ten, smokes American cigarettes, wears a bowler and a raincoat. What about your workshop man?"

"He's as old as I am. And takes snuff. The description fits young Grierson. But he's not a bad young chap. He's been with me for eight years." He shook his head. "Good lord—Mrs Courtenay dead. I can't believe it."

"It's true enough."

"But what makes you think it's young Grierson?"

"She lived alone with her maid. Never wore the jewels since she went blind twenty years ago. Maid had never seen them. They only left the flat once every two years to come here for cleaning. She knew the thief came from your shop."

"But how could she have told you? She's dead, you say."

"She was a gallant old lady. Blind, but not helpless. More than a match for your Grierson. He came in to her and, I imagine, there was some talk between them while she refused to hand over the key. And while they talked, unknown to him, she was making notes about him."

Burrows referred to his slip of paper and read, "Young man. Not gentleman. Bowler hat. Gloves. Raincoat. American cigarettes. Angry. Knows jewel details well. Walter in locket. Edith's hair in brooch. Must be from Munster and Son."

Burrows put the paper back in his pocket. "Yes, she was no fool. The room was in darkness. She was blind, but right under his nose she wrote it all down on the nice clean blotter on her desk. She wrote it in dots, sticking the point of her knitting needle into the soft blotting paper. Wrote it in dots, poor lady, just six dots that you can arrange into sixty-three combinations and which can tell you anything a blind person wants to tell you. Braille.

"I think you'd better send for young Grierson. Right under his nose—can you beat it? Tapping away with her knitting needle in the dark!"

Star Stuff

I SUPPOSE my real trouble is that I've never been able to resist a good cash proposition. Sometimes they turn up trumps. But more often not. Not that I mind. Life is full of ups and downs. When you're up you enjoy it and when you're down—well, you have the next up to look forward to.

You know Tania Lamont? Who doesn't? Tania Lamont in *Abruptly, With Love*. Tania Lamont in *Sleeping Wives*. Tania Lamont in this and in that, and right out there now, across the square, a great neon-lighted cut-out of her in a green sheath dress stretching halfway down the façade of the Paragon and a lot of pigmy faces staring up at her out of the rain. Star worship.

Well, I made her. I gave Tania Lamont her first break. Five years ago. But she was not called Tania Lamont when I first saw her. No, sir. But then a lot of things change when you get into the film business and the first—if you're a girl going places—is usually your name.

At the time I was assistant producer to Otto Heldmaster. It sounds good, doesn't it? The great Heldmaster. But it didn't amount to much. There were three assistant producers and all we did was to sit around waiting to be sent on errands, walk his black poodle, do this, do that—rarely anything of real importance.

Well, one evening he took me to the Savoy for dinner. Not because he liked me particularly, but because he wanted someone to talk to, and I happened to be around. I just sat opposite him and he went on and on about the new picture he had coming up. I didn't say much—Otto liked someone to talk at. It put him off if he were answered.

The great Heldmaster was about fifty, a big fleshy-faced man with a short mat of crisp black hair that looked like astrakhan, and small blue, rather watery eves that never seemed to blink. He talked about this new film and how some people wanted him to do it in colour and he was damned if lie would. People didn't care whether a film was in black and white, colour, or anything so long as it was a good film, and he made good films. Always had. Always would.

And he was damned too if he would take any of the stars they kept pushing at him. The right girl was around somewhere and he would find her and make her. I knew he would, too. He always found what he wanted and it wasn't any good trying to help him.

And then, slap in the middle of his filet mignon, he got up and said goodbye to me, getting my name wrong, and explaining that he must positively be in bed before ten as this was a bad period under his horoscope and he needed the utmost rest for the next three days. He meant it, too. He was a great one for horoscopes and the crystal ball, for never walking under a ladder, for touching wood—he used to carry a little piece of black mahogany in his breast pocket.

So I sat there alone with my thoughts and the prospect of paying the bill and arguing the next day with the accounts people about it because Otto would look blank and not even remember if he had been with me. Anyway, I finished my steak and passed on to coffee and with it the waiter brought a note asking me to join another table for liqueurs. He pointed out the table across the room. It had only one occupant, a dark-haired woman in a white dress with a sparkle about her neck and hands that looked expensive even at that distance.

I went over. When opportunity knocks, you always want to answer. She was in her early twenties, and even without the diamonds she could knock your eye out.

She said, “I saw Mr. Heldmaster leave you. I hope you didn’t resent my note,”

“I’m here,” I said. “Anyway, I’ve a feeling you’re more interested in Mr. Heldmaster than in me. But I warn you, though I’m perfectly willing to get you an interview with him, it won’t work. I’ve tried it before, for money and for love. He just likes to find his stars for himself.”

“I’m aware of that, Mr.—?”

“Speedwell, Jimmy.”

The waiter hovered. and after she had said Cointreau, I said Grand Marnier, and then I went on, to her, “I’m sorry—I can’t help.”

“I’m sure you can.” She smiled at me and it was a good smile. She had everything, including money. and I couldn’t think why she wanted more. But some women are like that.

“How?” I asked.

“I want to be a film star. It sounds terrible said like that, doesn’t it? But I do. And I’ll be frank. I don’t want to do years of dreary repertory work and so on for it. I want to go in at the top.”

“Who wouldn’t?”

But she gave me that smile again and there was a lot of calculation behind it. “It can be done. You know Mr. Heldmaster. From what I hear he always goes on hunches. Now, you find a way for him to discover me and I’ll pay you two thousand pounds the day he signs me to a contract. A hundred now, as a guarantee of good faith—and the understanding between us that our little arrangement remains a dead secret forever."

"With all due respect," I said, "I think you're crazy. I don't have any way of doing it."

She stood up. "You look to me like the kind of young man who can find a way. My name is Nicholson—Miss—and my telephone number is in this envelope with the hundred pounds." She dropped an envelope before me.

"You came here with this envelope all prepared?"

"I've got a good intelligence service. Mr. Heldmaster frequently dines here with one of his assistant producers."

She left, trailing a clutch of mink from one hand, and without looking back.

I slept on it for three nights. £2000. I was fed up with being an assistant producer. With £2000 I could take off for the South of France for six months and do that thing I really like doing—which is not having to work. And the when—I thought that there was no possible way—Otto handed it to on a platter.

He pushed his head round office door and called to me one afternoon, "Harry!"

"Jimmy, Mr. Heldmaster."

"Oh, yes, Jimmy. Ring Mrs. Zaremba and tell her I'd like to change my weekly appointment from Wednesday to Thursday the same time."

"Yes, sir."

But I didn't ring her. I went round to her flat in Chelsea. Zaremba, I was sure, wouldn't be offended at the prospect of £200. That kind of money doesn't float out of crystal balls when you tickle them.

I put it to her straight. She was a granite-chinned woman with a pair of eyes like black marbles and a gipsy scarf over her head—the kind I was sure, who didn't want any finessing about money.

I talked and she listened and occasionally she nodded, and there the table between us was her crystal ball with a velvet cloth over it.

When I'd finished she said, "You are in love with this girl, aren't you?"

"I am." She would have to do better with her crystal ball than that to get my personal trade. "Will you do it? Please." I even got a catch in my voice for her.

She nodded. "I will. Two hundred and fifty pounds. Fifty now. Two hundred more if it comes off."

Well, it was fifty more than I'd bargained for, but I agreed and went straight out and telephoned Miss Nicholson. There was no need to beat about the bush.

I said, "You know Mr. Heldmaster has a suite on the third floor of the Royal Curzon Hotel?"

"Yes.

"Well, by hook or by crook, and by this coming Thursday, I want you to take a suite on the floor below. Any suite on the second floor will do. But they all have different coloured entrance doors—blue, yellow, green, red, and so on. When you've got a suite just let me know the colour of the door, Can you do that?"

"If I have to buy the hotel."

"Good. Now, the next step. On Thursday you stay in that suite all afternoon—until midnight if necessary. Don't have a maid or anyone else in. Whoever knocks on the door, you answer it in person. Some time after four Mr. Heldmaster'll knock. Just pretend you don't know him. React how you like.

But he won't take anything from you except your signature on a contract. He'll discover you. Okay?"

"You're sure this is going to work?"

"It can't fail. It's a crystal-ball certainty."

It would be, too. Otto could be as keen as a hawk, but the fortune-telling stuff put blinkers on him, He'd held up production on his last film for two weeks because some star or planet was in the wrong house or quarter or something.

Well, I bit my nails until Otto went off for his appointment on Thursday. I'd got the message from Miss Nicholson that her door was a green one and had passed the information to Mrs. Zaremba.

I sat there imagining the interview. It wasn't hard—I'd done the script for it. I could hear her voice as she hung over the crystal ball and Otto lapped it all up … "Yes, something comes, the shadows draw back. I see you, Mr. Heldmaster, walking, walking through the streets, walking up to a hotel entrance and all about you there is a green aura—of thought, of worry, and I feel that you are waiting for guidance.

"Oh, how strong your vibrations are, glowing so green … You go through the lobby like a man in a dream, a green haze about you, you walk to the marble stairway—it's a lovely stairway with carved fish, big fish, at the bottom. You walk up to the second floor and you turn right and the doors of the suites stretch out before you.

"I can't see the numbers on them—but they are all different colours, But like a man in a dream, compelled by your own destiny, you go straight to the green door and you knock …

"Oh, dear, it begins to fade … No, no, I see the door open and a young, dark-haired, beautiful woman stands there—a stranger to you—and on your face I see a sudden blaze of revelation. This girl is the answer—the answer to your problem. Oh, it's going fast. The crystal ball is getting clouded ..."

The marble stairway in Otto's hotel, the Royal Curzon, had two carved dolphins at the foot. It couldn't miss.

And that is how Otto found the girl for his next film. At five o'clock I got a call from an excited Otto to bring a cameraman over to his suite. We went over there. Otto's man let us in. In the lounge was Otto, and a dark-haired girl stood by the fireplace with her back to us.

Otto said, "This, gentlemen, is the young lady who is going to star in my next film. Under the influence of the stars, guided and inspired by my own aura as though in a soft green haze, I have been led to her."

The girl turned. She was dark-haired and lovely. But it wasn't Miss Nicholson.

Otto introduced her to us. "Miss Janet Bolton," he said. "But we'll change that. Just think, I found her in this hotel! —on the floor below where she worked as a secretary to an old lady who has a suite there."

Well, there it was. Less than a year later Janet Bolton was Tania Lamont.

As soon as I could get away rang Miss Nicholson. It was a brief interview. No one had knocked on her door.

I said, "What the hell happened then? He was still mumbling about his green aura when I left him. He must have knocked on your door."

"Nobody knocked, I tell you. That fool Mrs. Zaremba must have got it wrong."

"No, I've already checked with her. Green, she said. Green. And Otto's babbling green, too."

I could hear her breathing angrily over the telephone, then she snapped, "That damned fool Otto Heldmaster must be colour blind."

Although she didn't know it—and I didn't find out until an intimate friend of Otto's let it slip one night when he'd had too many brandies—Miss Nicholson was dead right. Otto had been colour blind all his life. That's why he'd never make colour films.

Green and red looked just the same to him. He'd simply knocked on the wrong door—a red one I checked later, and got the right girl—for there was no doubt about the girl. Tania Lamont had star stuff in her all the time—just take a look across the square in front of the Paragon.

Death Wore Green

THERE are some people, kind, honest and good-hearted, who seem to have no luck in life at all. Joe Barker was like that. He was a decent, unassuming Londoner of twenty-five with sandy hair, blue eyes, a square pleasant mouth and a firm conviction that nothing would ever go right for him.

No matter how hard he tried, he never seemed to keep a job long; and no matter how nice and polite he was to them he never seemed to keep a girl long. This last worried him because at heart he was longing to be a family man and to have a home of his own. One way and another he was always getting into trouble, or doing or saying the wrong thing. In the end he got quite used to it and was no longer surprised at his misfortunes.

It was no surprise to him, therefore, when he fell overboard from the *S.S. Baroda*, five days out of Manila, somewhere in the Pacific Ocean.

Joe had gotten a job aboard as a cook. Clearing up his galley late one night, he came on deck with a can of garbage, walked aft to the stern where a section of the guard rail had been taken out and pitched the rubbish overboard. It was a fine night, ablaze with stars, and Joe put the can down and lit a cigarette. Then, as he turned to bend down and pick up the can and go back to his galley, his foot slipped on some potato peelings that had spilled on the deck. The next minute he was overboard—as clean as a whistle and with no time to shout, and the splash he made was lost in the streaming wake from the *S.S. Baroda*'s screws.

By the time he came to the surface, cleared his mouth of salt water and began to shout, his ship was two hundred yards ahead and not a soul heard him. Joe trod water and watched the lights of his ship fade away into the darkness. He knew that it would be early the next morning before he was missed and, knowing what his luck was like, he guessed that they would never find him.

He was wearing a shirt and drill trousers and was barefooted. The only thing of value he had on him was a waterproof wrist watch which he had bought in Manila and of which he was very proud. He kept looking at the luminous dial of this to see how the time was going, and it seemed to go very slowly indeed. Long before dawn came, Joe knew that he was getting very tired and couldn't last much longer. He made gentle little movements of his hands to keep himself afloat and he thought of the wife and kids he would now never have, of the little business he would now never start, and he tried to figure out just who would really miss him and couldn't think of a soul.

Some time toward dawn he began to go a bit fuzzy in the head and kept imagining he could hear noises, voices calling and sounds of boats passing, but even in his exhausted state he had enough sense to know that it was only his fancy. Just as the sun edged above the far horizon and spread the sea with a silver and gold sparkle of light, Joe lost consciousness.

When he came round he felt for a moment that the whole thing had been a dream which was still going on. He was lying on his back on a beach and feeling very ill. The sun, high in the sky now, was baking his clothes dry. Over his head palm trees tossed their spear leaves in a gentle wind, and distantly he could hear the noise of waves breaking over some reef.

Crowding around him were six native girls. They were jabbering away among themselves, highly excited, and sometimes touching him as though they weren't really convinced that he existed. As for Joe, he was considerably embarrassed. The girls were as beautiful a bunch as he had seen in his life, but their idea of dress seemed to be a grass skirt and a few hibiscus flowers stuck in their hair.

Joe blushed and shut his eyes. He felt himself propped up by a soft arm, and a drinking shell was pressed against his lips. He opened his eyes and drank, and the girls nodded and clapped their hands approvingly. The one who was propping him up had a much lighter skin than the others. She smiled at him, wrinkled her pretty nose, and he saw that her eyes were brown with flecks of gold in them. Joe smiled back and kept his eyes strictly on her face. It seemed the polite thing to do and saved him embarrassment.

However, Joe's embarrassment was something he had to learn to live with. After a time four native men appeared carrying a litter with a canopy of palm leaves, and Joe was loaded aboard and borne in style from the beach to a small village. He was put in a hut, given food and coconut wine; and because the wine was strong he fell asleep, hoping that when he woke again the whole thing would not turn out to be a dream.

It didn't; and by the next day Joe knew where he was and what it was all about. He had been pulled out of the sea by the six girls who had been out fishing in a canoe, and he was on a small atoll named Alifa which was one of the Caroline Islands and well off any trade routes. Not for twenty years had a white man been to the island. But that wasn't the reason why Joe was such a sensation. The explanation was given to him by an old man called Raua who had once been a mission boy in New Guinea and spoke some English.

"On Alifa," he said, "always plenty more women than men. Six girls who rescue you have no young men to marry. All want be bride to you."

"What? All six?" Joe's eyes widened.

"No, no. We good people. One man, one wife. You marry one girl from six. New blood, new babies, maybe plenty boy babies. Not like last time. Gods send white stranger from the sea. He pick bride of gods, but only have damn girl babies. so, women put him in boat and send him away … Maybe drowned. Perhaps sharks eat."

"You really mean I'm expected to marry one of these six girls?" Joe couldn't get over it.

"Damn sure."

Joe, for the first time in his life, felt that his luck was turning. Usually girls wouldn't look at him. Now he had six to choose from. At this moment Joe's eye fell on Lei-lei who came up to the but with his midday drink of coconut wine. She was the lighter skinned girl whom he had first noticed on the beach, and much more since.

Although all the young girls looked after him and treated him like a king, Lei-lei went out of her way more than the others to see he had everything. There was no doubt about it that she had taken a fancy to him; and, if the truth had to be known, Joe had taken a fancy to her.

"Well," said Joe, "it won't be difficult to pick the girl I want."

Raua shook his head. "Very difficult to pick. Six girls all want you. No can agree which have you. So, young girls go up to mountain top and dance for gods. Then gods say which one will be bride. Always same thing when more than one girl want same man."

"Doesn't the man get any say in this?" asked Joe indignantly.

"Damn sure, no. Women run things on Alifa. After gods pick bride, young girls come down and dance for you. You pick right one, if not …"

"If not, what?"

"Everyone take spears and kill you, or gods get angry,"

"What?" Joe frowned. "But how am I expected to know which one to pick?"

Raua's wrinkled old face split with a sly grin. "You pay Raua well. He tell you when time come how to pick bride of gods. Women no want young man killed. They make plan with Raua. Give sign. Very easy."

"But I've got no money. How can I pay you?"

Raua chuckled. "Fine watch you wear. You make present to Raua? Damn sure, yes?"

Joe handed over his watch.

There were two weeks to go before the new moon and the bride-picking ceremony. In those days Joe and Lei-lei saw a lot of each other. They went for walks together and Joe taught her a little English, and she told him that she was the daughter of the last white visitor, a Scots engineer who had fallen overboard drunk from his ship. In no time at all Joe had lost his heart to her, and Lei-lei felt the same way about Joe. On the night before the new moon they walked on the beach together, and Joe slipped his arm around her waist.

"If you're not elected, lass," said Joe, "I don't know what I'll do. No, that's not honest. No man wants his back full of spears. Oh, damn!"

Lei-lei looked up at him tenderly, "Lei-lei love Joe. Joe love Lei-lei, Gods maybe pick Lei-lei for bride,"

"Not if I know my luck ..." sighed Joe.

At noon the next day them was a ceremonial feast, suckling pig, fish, taros, bananas, breadfruit and plenty of coconut wine. Afterward the six young girls, singing and dancing, filed away into the jungle toward the mountain that dominated the little island. Joe waited under a palm tree, and the rest of the village sat around polishing and sharpening their spears, full of good humor for they were sure that Raua would tip the young white man off which girl to pick.

As dusk began to fall, the sound of singing was heard from the jungle, and then into the village clearing came the procession of young girls, all carrying torches. Joe, sitting on a dais in the center of the clearing with Raua beside him, said, "Come on, Raua—how do I tell?" He was overanxious, angry and a little tipsy from too much coconut wine. Fine thing that a man couldn't choose his own wife!

Raua said, "Very easy. Raua, he arrange sign. All girls wear grass skirts, each different color, green, yellow, so on—but bride of gods wear red skirt." And with that Raua slipped away.

Joe sat there with Raua's words ringing in his head. Pick the girl with the red skirt. But how could he?

"Hey, Raua!" he shouted for the old man, but Rana was lost among the dancers. Wasn't it just like his luck, thought Joe, his heart sinking as he saw the villagers, spears in hand, watching him. For any other man to pick out the one girl among the six in a red skirt would have been easy. But not for Joe. One of the things that had always embarrassed him, could even have been the reason for a certain inferiority complex in him, was the fact that he was colour blind and couldn't tell red from green. All reds looked green to him.

The young girls swirled round him, clapping their hands and swaying, all of them wearing grass skirts and garlands of flowers. Wilder and wilder grew the dance, and then suddenly with a great shout they stopped and stood silently before him. Joe rose, his eyes sweeping along the row. There was a cold sweat on his brow. For the life of him he couldn't tell which was wearing the red skirt. Out of the six girls he eliminated four, but both the last two seemed to him to be wearing green. And Lei-lei was one of the two. But did she have the red skirt or the other? Then, because he loved Lei-lei. Joe stepped down, said a silent prayer to himself that he might be right, and took her by the hand,

The next moment, from the howl of rage that went up from all the other women and the sudden flash of spear tips in the torchlight, he knew that he had chosen wrong.

Lei-lei saved him. Site turned and ran for the jungle, dragging Joe with her. Joe never understood how they made it, but they did. Lei-lei went like the wind and he followed. Half an hour later the sound of pursuit was far behind them and, when they reached the other side of the island, Lei-lei Found a fishing canoe and they pushed off into the darkness. Two days later a liner picked them up.

They keep a little restaurant now, and a more devoted couple it would be hard to find. They've got two boys and a girl, and when the kids are in bed at night Lily Barker looks across at her Joe thinking what a wonderful man he is. The bravest in the world … the kind of man who for love of her defied the island gods and risked death from her peoples' spears.

And Joe, for his part, has become expert at hiding his colour blindness. Although he loves her with all his heart, he has had the good sense not to tell her the truth behind his choice. After all, in the happiest marriage, there's no harm in keeping some things to yourself.

The Aberdyll Onion

ALTHOUGH it was only eleven o'clock in the morning, Sir John gave me a glass of whisky and a cigar as thick as a broom handle, and sat me down in a great leather armchair.

"Hughes," he said to me, "how long have you lived in Aberdyll?"

"Seventy years," I said. He knew it as well as I did, but Sir John was a great one for telling and asking people things. Little, fat chap he was, with a bald head and a ginger moustache, and a temper to go with it. I wish I had all the money he's made out of Aberdyll Onion Soup, Aberdyll Welsh Broth, Aberdyll Asparagus Tips, and so on, and all in tins.

"And not a thing goes on here but that you don't know all or something about it, eh?"

I nodded. "More or less, Sir John."

"And that's why I asked you to come up here, Hughes. Got a little job for you. Fifty pounds if you bring it off. A little detective work."

"Wouldn't that be more in the line of Jones the Police?" I asked.

"P.C. Jones? No. Good fellow, but he could be in it. Never know what a man will do when it comes to horticultural pride. He's after the Aberdyll Cup, too, you know."

"Ah," I said. "About the onion is it, then?"

"It is, Hughes. Some scoundrel has stolen Williams's onion. Two years he's won my cup, and from what I could see was likely to win it again this year. That would give him the cup for good and five hundred pounds. Wonderful publicity it would be for our soups."

Sir John ran on a bit, telling me about the Aberdyll Onion Cup as though I knew nothing about it. Every year there was a great competition for this cup at the Aberdyll Show. But more than that, Sir John used it for publicity for his tinned soups.

The Aberdyll Onion was something special. In all the papers each year. Entries limited to amateur growers in Aberdyll. Always a good deal of feeling about it in Aberdyll. Sometimes you'd get so that you didn't want to hear another word about onions … the right soil and fertilizers, and so on. Well—some of the chaps used to sit up at nights with their onions, talking to them, maybe … egging them on.

"Keep your ear to the ground, make some inquiries, Hughes," Sir John was saying now, "Let me know what scoundrel took Williams's onion. I'll make him regret it."

And he would, too, with that old temper and a J.P., too. So I promised to do what I could and went off to see Williams the Onion—that's what they call him, seeing he'd won the cup twice and had looked like winning it outright.

Dark, quiet young chap he was, strong chapel man, a porter on the railway, and a broken-hearted man. That onion might have been his favourite child.

"I'm telling you, man," he said, "it was in the garden at half past seven. I was working there. And then I come in for a bite of supper"—he's a bachelor and looks after himself in a bit of a cottage behind the station—"and go out again at half past eight just to see it's all right and maybe cover it from the heavy dew, and it's gone. A real shock. Day before yesterday it was. Big as a football almost. There's a lovely colour it was, too."

"Who would you say had the nearest chance of beating you?" I asked him.

"Let's see now. Jones the Police might. Then there's Morgan the Waterworks. And Evans the Pub. Nobody else would have a chance. My own seed, you know. Special. Nothing left now but a big hole dug clean in the ground, man. No doubt whatever, whoever did it took all that soil so they could analyse it and find out my secret feeding. I just can't go through the garden now, Hughes, bach …"

"No footprints in the soil?"

"Nothing. They could stand on the concrete path and dig it up."

Well, I went along first of all to Jones the Police's place. He was out on his beat, but Mrs Jones, a sharp little woman with four children, opened the door to me and out with it came a delicious smell of stew, rich and oniony. But as I sniffed at it Mrs. Jones said to me, a little quick like: "Our own onions, Mr. Hughes, and between half past seven and half past eight the night before last Jones was watching the telly with me and the kids. And now, if you'll pardon me, I'll have to go and take that stew off before it burns."

With Morgan up at the waterworks it was different. He invited me in and gave me a glass of beer and said: "Hughes, bach, I'm a timid man. All my life I've lacked courage. Big dreams have been my share, but only little actions. That's why I read so much. I live in the imagination, man. I lack the courage to live in the real world."

He went on: "We Morgans are poets. Dreamer not doers. Otherwise I might have stolen Williams's onion. Think of it, man—a soft summer night, full of the smell of the warm earth, shadows, a solitary light from a cottage window and me, spade in hand, stealing like cut-throat through the gloom … There's a picture, look you." He put his hands in front of him and said: "Put the handcuffs on me, lead me away to prison and I'll write the Ballad of Aberdyll Jail."

Well, poet he might be, but a little drunk always was, and he didn't have to tell me that between half past seven and half past eight on the night he'd been down at the Aberdyll Arms.

And that's where I went to see Evans the Pub. I went in the back way, which is along a dark little passage, and as I passed through the door someone coming out bumped into me. It was young Phillips the Rolls, that is Sir John's chauffeur—a good-looking, well set up young fellow with fair hair.

I said: "If you're going up to the Hall to drive Sir John out somewhere, Phillips, you'd better wipe the lipstick off your face." Slap in middle of his right cheek it was, and he looked proper foolish.

Half-way down the passage, Nancy Evans was tidying her hair in a wall mirror. Now you couldn't miss Nancy, dark, all curves and as good-natured as a spaniel. I pinched her bottom and went into the bar and she went round behind the counter and pulled me my usual glass of half-and-half. As she handed it to me she said: "That's thirty shillings you've got on the slate, Mr. Hughes."

"I'm expecting a legacy at the end of the week," I said. "Where's your da?"

"In Cardiff where he has been these last three days—so if you're snooping around about the old onion you can forget it. My da wouldn't do such a thing."

"Your da," I said, "would give you a tanning if he caught you kissing young Phillips. And so would Williams the Onion. I thought you two were promised?"

"We've been walking out for three years. It's a long promise. And young Phillips is a mannerly chap."

"If Williams won the cup this year, he'd have five hundred pounds. More than enough to set up a house," I said. "If someone didn't want you and him to marry, look you, it's tempted to pinch the old onion they might be to give themselves more time to get you to change your mind."

"If pigs had wings, they'd fly."

"And where were you between half past seven and half past eight night before last?"

"Looking for gold at the foot of the rainbow, Mr. Hughes." She was a saucy piece but I liked her.

"And where was young Phillips?"

"How should I know?"

"Then I must have been dreaming," I said, "because on my way here that night I could have sworn I seen him and you sitting on the railway embankment, not far from Williams's cottage. The foot of that rainbow must have been mighty narrow for you were both squeezed very tight to get under it."

"At your age," said Nancy, "you want glasses."

"I see well enough. Still, though the onion's been stolen, no harm's done."

"What's that?" she asked.

"Williams is no fool. He means to get that cup and the money. I wouldn't tell you this if you weren't practically his fiancée, but he's got another little patch of ground up behind the rectory. He's been growing another prize onion there in secret."

I finished my beer and went out and I when I was safely away I couldn't help chuckling at the memory of Nancy's face. I may be old, but there's nothing you can teach me about love.

It was as clear as day that Nancy didn't want to marry Williams any more, and that between her and young Phillips they had done away with the onion. All I had to do was to watch in the little bit of ground behind the rectory that warm summer night and I was sure that either Nancy or Phillips would appear to steal the other onion.

So, just before dark I got up to the little bit of ground by the rectory and made myself comfortable between a couple of gooseberry bushes.

I waited there for about two hours and then things began to happen. There was a noise at the far end of the ground, and then another at my end, and then right across the way from me I heard somebody stumble against a wheelbarrow.

I stood up and switched on a torch and swung it round in a circle. First of all I saw young Nancy and Phillips, blinking in the light like a couple of young owls. Then, swaying by the wheelbarrow was Morgan the Waterworks, and away on my left was Jones the Police.

I gave a little laugh and shook my head. Pretty sheepish they all looked.

"Welcome friends," I said. "Nancy's been talking in the pub, is it? And you've all come to steal the onion."

P.C. Jones, who was in uniform, drew himself up and said with dignity, "I'm here to protect it. Same as you, bach."

Morgan comes weaving across to me. his eyes shining, and said: "Morgan becomes a doer. Found my courage at last, man. I've come for that onion."

"So have Nancy and I," said young Phillips, with his arms round Nancy. "And we would have taken the first if we'd thought of it. We love each other and she don't want to go through with it with Williams. Can't see any girl wanting to be known as Mrs. Williams the Onion for the rest of her life."

"That's right," said Nancy. "Mrs. Phillips the Rolls for me. I love him."

I looked around at them all and then I said: "You'd better all go home and I'll forget about this. Williams hasn't got a second onion up here."

You should have seen their faces. Anyway, after a bit of argument they left. But I sat there a while, thinking like. Then I went to see Williams.

"Williams," I said, "there's practising a deceit you've been."

"Go away, Hughes, bach," he said. "I am on the horns of a dilemma."

"True," I said. "Proper stuck, too, you are." I told him what I had done, and I finished: "But none of the people that come up to the rectory had so much as a spade in their hands. They were going to pull up the onion. But your own was dug up. The work of a true onion lover who couldn't bear to damage so much as a hair of a root."

I walked to a little recess in the corner of the kitchen and pulled the curtain back. There, planted neat and beautiful in the centre of a wooden tub, was the onion. Man, it was a size.

"Why did you do it?" I asked.

He shook his head. "It's this dilemma," he said. "If I'd have won the prize this year I'd have got five hundred pounds, and then I would have had to marry Nancy. We're promised."

"And you don't want to marry her?"

"No, man, I don't. She's a nice enough girl. But my heart is with that old onion and everything that grows. What I want is to take that five hundred and start a nursery garden business with it. That would mean a lot of hard work and no time until much later for marriage. But I'm a man of honour—"

I said: "Williams, bach, if you'd had eyes for anything but your onion you'd have saved yourself a lot of trouble. Put it back and win the prize. You don't have to break your word to Nancy. She wants to marry Phillips the Rolls. She don't want to be Mrs. Williams the Onion."

"She don't?"

"Put it back and I'll tell Sir John some story that'll cover it for you and also do me no harm so far as my fifty pounds is concerned."

You should have seen the way he went over and lifted that tub so lovingly. Once a man like Williams falls in love with a vegetable, his eyes are closed to all women.

The White Spell

HARRY'S Bar is in Venice and the two of us were drinking martinis. He said he was an Australian sheep farmer on his way to England, and his voice had a lot of Welsh in it. And, of course, there was the dog. It had strayed in out of the heat and we were feeding it occasional potato crisps.

My friend had sad, romantic eyes, a humorous mouth and a wallet that bulged inside his silk jacket. He gave the dog a pat and said, "Somewhere in him I swear there's a touch of Welsh sheep dog. In fact, if I shut my eyes and squint and pretend that he's black and white instead of brown, he could be the dead spit of Jason."

"And who was Jason?" I asked.

"A dog," he said. "The best. I'll tell you about him. As quick as a mountain stream, as quiet as night, a clever as the devil, and what he didn't know about sheep you could have written on an ear of corn …"

High poetry and a more pronounced Welsh accent came into his voice as he got going. In the little Welsh hill town of Llanidor, it seemed, there were three brothers; John Evans, twenty-four and the eldest; Idris Evans, twenty-three; and then Morgan Evans, the youngest, twenty-two, and they were the sons of a well-to-do sheep farmer. Each brother had a sheep dog, but Jason belonged to John and the dogs of the other brothers couldn't compare with it. Each year when the town held its local show it was John with Jason who won the sheep dog trials.

Now the rivalry of the brothers over their dogs was innocent enough. Less innocent, however, was their rivalry over a woman.

"It's in love they all were," said my friend. "Hopelessly, fightingly in love with a woman. Her name was Helen and more beautiful than that other who put the cat among the pigeons at Troy or wherever it was."

He went on for some time, about Helen, but finally came round to the point. The Evans brothers would all inherit well from their father who owned several farms and Helen, while she didn't favour one more than the other, let it be seen that it was between one of them and the son of Williams, the pub. The pub, in fact, was a fine hotel—the Llanidor Arms and worth having.

Then one day young Williams was put right out of the running. The three Evans brothers had been up in the hills going over their sheep for fly and foot-rot and, on their way home, feeling hot and tired they stripped off by the side of a stream and bathed. After their swim they lay down naked in the grass in the sun and went to sleep.

Well, after a time they were awakened by the sound of someone singing. It was a woman's voice and, since they were naked, the young men sat up very quietly and cautiously and looked round.

"The sight that met their eyes," said my friend, "was idyllic, classical, right out of Daphnis and Chloë and there wasn't a man in Llanidor, or anywhere else for that matter, who wouldn't have given fifty pounds for the privilege which was theirs.

"In the middle of the pool, and the drought of summer had made it run shallow, was Helen. She was standing there as God made her, and as she sang to herself she was lifting the cool water in her hands and pouring it over the fairest body in the Principality of Wales and far beyond. The Evans brothers just sat there and watched the flash of water like quicksilver on her fair skin and the golden stream of her hair over her shoulders."

And then Helen had seen them. But she was a girl of great self-control. She crouched down until the water came to her shoulders and she said firmly, "John Evans, Idris Evans, and you, too, is it, Morgan Evans—I'll thank you all to shut your eyes until I'm out of this pool."

They did as they were told. When she had disappeared they put on their own clothes like men in a dream. In a few moments she came round to them, dressed now, and carrying herself like a queen.

"You've seen me mother naked," said Helen, who was not a girl to mince her words and could cast a column of figures more accurately and quickly than any bank clerk. "That's a thing should rest between man and wife. If I married anyone else in the valley now, as might be Williams the pub, you'd go round the rest of your lives with a knowing twitch to your lips and a snigger in your hearts. It's only human. Fortunately, I like you all well enough and now one of you must marry me."

"I'll brain them both if they so much as breathe it once we're married," said John, turning on the other two.

"I'll go to Cardiff for the ring tomorrow," said Idris squaring up to John.

"You stood in the water like a nymph," said Morgan dreamily. "Even the birds forgot to sing when they saw you. We'll go straight to the minister now and arrange the banns."

In another moment they would all have been at one another. But Helen had her own method for choosing which one it should be.

"I like you all," she said. "Not a pin between you. And I'll have no fighting over the matter. I'll marry the one of you who wins the sheep dog trials."

John Evans was content enough with this. He'd won the trials for the last three years. But the other two were in their different ways, determined to stop him from winning the trial this year. Idris was originally for poisoning Jason, but the dog would only take food from John and for every minute of the next two weeks John kept Jason with him night and day. Idris in the end got a new dog for which he paid fifty pounds and spent the time remaining to him working it. Morgan, who was no poisoner of dogs and too fond of his own little bitch, Meg, to change her, went to Widow Pandy who was by way of being a part-time witch and asked her help.

"Is it a spell that looks natural or sudden death for Jason you want?" she asked. "The first is more expensive."

"A natural spell," said Morgan.

"A hundred pounds, then," said Widow Pandy. "It's an amount I need badly. I will give you a white spell."

"Any sum, whatever," said Morgan dreamily. "Helen is beyond price."

"To be paid the day after your marriage and not a thing will you have to do, Morgan Evans, but work your dog Meg in the trials as always."

Well, the great day came, blistering hot and a fine crowd to watch the sheep dog finals.

The way the trial was worked was this; a flock of sheep was penned at the top of a long furze-spangled slope of hill. A handler let five of them out of the pen and from the bottom of the hill the shepherd sent away his dog to collect them and bring them down. On the way down they had to be passed through two hurdle gates, and then one sheep had to be shed—that is, left behind—and the four remaining brought on and penned in a small hurdle corral at the bottom of the hill.

Including the Evans brothers there were six shepherds in the final, but everyone knew it was going to be between the brothers. The three outsiders turned in good times. Then Morgan's turn came and when the sheep were loosed he sent away Meg. She shed one and had the other four penned in eight minutes fourteen seconds. Good time, but not championship stuff.

Then came Idris's turn with his new dog. He shed the first sheep in fine time but after that the whole thing went to pieces. One of the sheep was plain stubborn and awkward. So he went roaring up to the judges and shouted that the awkward sheep must have been blind.

"Blind, man!" laughed John Evans. "Look you, it's your dog that's blind."

Then came John's turn. John Evans—and you should have seen the dark scowl on his face—did worse than Idris. He never even got to shedding the first sheep, let alone penning four at the bottom of the hill. Jason, the dog, did all that a dog could do; but a couple of those sheep wandered and trotted around like drunken sailors. Oh, there was hell to pay! John finally gave up and went storming up to the judges. Two of his sheep were blind, he swore. But the judges wouldn't have it. They examined the sheep and found nothing wrong with them—and so they named Morgan the winner. Naturally, there was a bit of a fight after that, you know, between the brothers. But in the end Morgan wedded his Helen. And he paid the hundred pounds to Widow Pandy who needed it because her son wanted to emigrate to Australia and become a sheep farmer. Which he did. And fine and prosperous he became."

He pulled out his bulging wallet and called for two more martinis.

"And you," said I, seeing through him easily, "are Widow Pandy's son? How did the spell, work then?"

"Widow Pandy's son? Ah, yes—he worked the spell for her. He was handling the sheep at the top of the hill. When he let Idris's lot out he smacked a good dab of his mother's butter in the eye of one beast. And he did the same for two of John's beasts. This blinded them in one eye for about five minutes, but by the time the judges got to them the butter had run and looked like sweat in the fleece around their eyes and they could see well enough. But I'm not Widow Pandy's son. He has the next place to me in Australia. I'm Morgan Evans, look you. After two years with Helen I couldn't stand her any longer and I left her and emigrated."

Dialogue Behind a Curtain

THE Great Man stood at the window of the Winter Palace.

Across the paved courtyard, beyond the long sweep of ornamental railings and the still line of grey-uniformed guards, lay the wide bowl of the only harbour the island possessed. He raised a hand and scratched the back of his neck and the movement made the early morning November sun glint on the gilt oak leaves of his epaulettes.

A respectful three paces behind him the Chief of Police stirred uncomfortably and said, "That's his boat coming in now. For a year this has been going on, and until now we have never known which of the many fishermen it might be. This time our information is reliable."

"Denunciation?" The word was harsh and bitter.

"Yes."

"Anonymous?"

"Yes."

"You have suspected him?"

"He and every other fisherman on the island, but until now I would have said that he was the last man—"

The figure at the window turned and a pair of cold, brown eyes regarded the Chief of Police shrewdly. They were eyes which missed nothing.

"You sound almost regretful. You like him?"

"Everyone on the island likes Tasso."

The Great Man walked past the Chief of Police towards his desk and from the shadow of the curtains at the window rose the brown and black length of his great Alsatian. As his master sat down the dog dropped heavily to the floor at the side of the desk.

"Your men are waiting for him?"

"Everything is ready."

"Go down yourself and arrest him and bring him here. Do not question him. Say nothing to him. Bring him here."

The face of the Chief of Police showed his surprise. A large hand with a thick gold ring waved at him, and the ghost of a smile passed across the face of the Great Man. "Bring him here. For once I have time on my hands. I am curious to talk to a man who has found a soft corner in the heart of a Chief of Police. Such men are rare."

The Chief of Police would have spoken again but the cold, brown eyes had grown colder and the ghost of a smile had gone from the other's face. The Chief of Police saluted and left the room.

The Great Man lit a cigarette, eased his short powerful bulk back into the wide chair, and his left hand dropped to the neck of the Alsatian, the squat fingers teasing at the dog's thick fur. After a while there was the clatter of heavy boots on the wide marble stairway outside the room and then the door was opened. Tasso stood on the threshold, behind him two armed guards and behind them the Chief of Police. The Great Man eyed them in silence for a while and, in the long pause, the cries of the stallholders from the market along the quay front seeped faintly into the gilt and velvet stretches of the room.

"Let him come in alone," he said suddenly.

THE DOORS closed behind Tasso and the fisherman came slowly down the room. The dog by the chairside stirred, beginning to rise, but the firm fingers tapped its head gently and the animal relaxed.

Tasso stood before the polished desk. He was a short, powerful man, much like the other in build. His eyes were brown, but with a warmth in them, his face tanned and creased with years of the sea, and about the wide lips clung a subdued smile. He showed no fear, nor embarrassment, though he knew well the identity of the man before him, had seen him resplendent at ceremonial parades and known those cold, brown eyes from a thousand photographs in a thousand public places. He stood there with his shabby blue jacket swung open to show a dirty red shirt, his trousers flaked with fish scales. In the lapel of his jacket he wore a half-opened yellow rose.

"Your name?"

"Tasso Susvid."

"Age?"

"Fifty-three."

"Occupation?"

"Fisherman."

"And smuggler."

"No man willingly puts his initials on a bullet." The frank eyes watched the smoke rising from the other's cigarette.

"You have been denounced."

"The innocent as well as the guilty are often denounced."

The Great Man stirred comfortably and the ghost of a smile came back. "Let us assume that you are a smuggler for the moment."

"Why not? I have time on my hands. My fish are caught and my wife will sell them."

"Why do you smuggle? It is against the interests of our country."

"If I do it—and we merely pass time with this game—it is to make myself more money. The better off the citizens of a country are, the better off the country."

"There are times when you smuggle out enemies of our country. A man who does that merits death."

"Why not a reward? Surely, a country is healthier without its enemies?"

The lips of the Great Man tightened and for a moment his eyes narrowed. Then he laughed gently.

"What do you bring in so valuable that it outweighs the risk of death?"

"Cigarettes."

"We make our own."

"But the one you smoke now is American."

"What else?"

"Whiskey."

"I prefer our own rakia."

"I agree, but there are people in the capital who think differently. There are also nylons and perfumes."

"For the women in the capital?"

Tasso smiled. and shook his head. "For any woman. Every goat girl on this island covets a pair of nylons, and if you tend goats you have need of perfumes."

The Great Man smiled, almost openly now, and said, "And all these things you bring from over there?" He nodded towards the window and blue patch of visible sea.

"If I were a smuggler I should bring them from there, yes."

"How long would it take—in your boat?"

"Ten hours across, four hours there, and ten hours back. Twenty-four hours."

"When did you go out on this fishing trip?"

"At nine o'clock yesterday morning."

The Great Man glanced at the clock over the wide doors of the saloon. "It is now half-past nine. It's odd—your trip lasted exactly twenty-four hours."

"I ran into bad weather last night and we had to heave-to."

"We?"

"My son works the boat with me."

"Your boat is being searched now."

"They will find nothing."

"You have a radio? Maybe someone warned you—"

"There is no radio. No one warned me. Remember, we are only pretending that I am a smuggler."

"It is a game not without its dangers. During the war, you were a partisan?"

"Yes, I fought. Later, because I know the coast, I was a pilot for the Allied naval forces."

"You like the English?"

"They understand the sea, and they keep their heads in an emergency. Both qualities I admire."

"Who doesn't? But even so, everything is passing from their grasp. In politics, in art, in commerce and in sport they are being swallowed up."

Tasso shrugged his shoulders. "In all these things, perhaps. But I like them still because of all these the one thing they will really care about is sport. Only being able to draw with our National football team yesterday—they will find that hard to swallow."

"You are interested in football?"

"Every man on this island is. My son is captain of the town team."

"He will be proud when you are shot for smuggling."

"The bullet has yet to be marked. Remember, this is a private game between us."

"You have been denounced. The game is finished."

"Denounced by whom?"

"I don't know, but I should say your wife."

"Why?"

"She is a woman. Women notice small things…" A large hand rubbed gently across a broad jowl for a moment and the thick gold ring caught the light from the wide windows. "Four hours over there is not long, but it is long enough for a man to forget his wife. You wear a fresh rose in your lapel. A man who lands from sea after twenty-four hours with a fresh rose in his coat gives himself away. After a ten hour trip from over there it would be fresh. Maybe you have made this mistake before. Maybe your wife has noticed it and grown jealous of the one who pins a flower to your coat before you leave. Jealousy makes all women dangerous. Yes, I think it was your wife who denounced you."

Tasso smiled and raised his hand to the rose. "I am fifty-three. At thirty-three my wife was often jealous, but those years have gone. We are still playing our game. Look—" Tasso tossed the rose on to the desk. The movement made the Alsatian rise quickly, but a broad hand went out to restrain it. The Great Man picked up the rose and saw that it was artificial, made of wax-coated silk.

Tasso said, "It was the gift of an American nurse during the war. Ask any man in this town and he will tell you that I always wear it. After six years it is still fresh."

The great man was silent for a moment, turning the rose over in his hand. Then he looked up from under his heavy brows and smiled.

"A man who holds my power can resent the mistakes he makes. Out of hurt vanity I might take revenge and none would question my right. A snap of my fingers and our friend here …" he nodded to the Alsatian, "would tear your throat out. Maybe I should let him for you are too frank and your tongue too ready."

But the smile still played about Tasso's mouth and he slowly raised his hand to the back of his neck, saying, "If you should try—there would be two throats cut. The dog's and your own." From the back of his coat he pulled a knife and placed it on the desk. "The Chief of Police is a conscientious man, but your presence here flusters him. He was so anxious to get me up here that he made a bad job of searching me."

The Great Man picked up the knife and gently tried the edge of the blade on his thumb. Then he said, reflectively, "There are a thousand men who would have liked the chance you've just thrown away."

"I am a fisherman, not an assassin."

"And also a smuggler. Some instinct told you to jettison your goods before coming in."

"I am a fisherman."

"No. I may have been mistaken about your wife, but not over the smuggling. Yesterday you were over there."

Tasso shook his head. "I was at sea—hove-to."

The Great Man went on, turning the knife in his hands as he spoke, "You left this island yesterday morning with your son. According to you, you have been twenty-four hours at sea, seeing no one and without a radio of any kind."

"That is what I said."

"And you landed here a little less than half-an-hour ago and were brought straight up to me without a chance to talk to anyone?"

"That is so."

"And yet you knew that our International Football team had drawn with the English team? The game was played in London yesterday afternoon, after you left here. You heard the result over there when you landed. Both you and your son would be interested in the result. If you had been at sea twenty-four hours without a radio you could not have known the result. It is forbidden to go over there, but you went as you have so often gone."

Tasso's face never altered. For a moment the two men stared at one another. Then Tasso nodded slowly. "The game, it seems, is finished."

But the Great Man smiled and shook his head. "No. I have enjoyed the game too much to have it finish this way." He stood up. "You are free to go. What I know I shall keep to myself, and you will have no trouble with the Chief of Police."

"Why do you do this?" Tasso's face showed his surprise.

The other put his hand for a moment on Tasso's shoulder.

"You made a mistake, one mistake that could have meant death. That can happen to the bravest and cleverest of men. It might happen to me one day. If it does, I shall know I have a friend on this island with a boat. A man can never have too many friends."

Watch Your Step

FATHER ROSARIO and I came down the hill together towards the little port. It had rained during the night and the colours were fresh and vivid. The blue sea sparkled below us, the pink and white houses crowding round the square were bright in the sun, and behind us the tawny hills were studded with the jet shadows cast by the olive trees. To our right brawled the mountain stream, in spate from the rain which had been heavy in the hills. And it all looked the same as it had done eleven years before, when I had been in uniform and not on holiday, and the hills behind us had been full of Germans.

"We are glad to have you back, my son," said Father Rosario. "You will find little changed here, except that there is more to eat, and the men are all at home."

When I had known it last, food had been the big problem, and most of the men had been away in the hills, fighting as partisans.

"I've always wanted to come back, Father. Many times in the past years I've promised myself that one day I should be out there in the bay, fishing. And that I should see you again."

He gave a little nod of his head, a lean, black-robed figure at my side, and I wondered if he knew that it was he who had brought me back. He was a man for whom I had an immense respect, a man of great courage and greater wisdom … but beyond these he had something else, a warm humanity and a gentle understanding of men. He was old and he was thin, and he looked as though a wind would blow him away, a harsh word wither him, but I knew differently.

"We shall ask Giorgio about the fishing." He motioned with his hand towards a small cottage on the left. "He lives there, but at the moment he will be down with the boats. You will not remember Giorgio for he was away during your time here. His wife died just after the war and he now lives alone. He is a fine man, but a little intemperate."

Down below the cottage there was a row of stepping-stones across the stream. Father Rosario gathered up his robe and went across, and. I followed, the water washing over the stones and almost into my shoes. We came to the first of the houses, went down a small alleyway whose walls were overgrown with bougainvillaea and, turning a corner, were in the square. It was quiet and peaceful and on the far side, beyond a low wall, lay the sea.

As we crossed to the wall, there floated up to us, from the sands below, the sound of men's voices raised in argument.

Father Rosario and I leaned over. Small fishing-boats were drawn up on the beach, and some children were bathing from the end of a ramshackle jetty. Below us, gathered about a pile of nets, were five men. Four of them squatted on the sand, working at the nets, and the fifth, a burly, blue-shirted figure, black-haired, his skin burnt a fine mahogany, stood beyond them, shouting angrily, making himself heard above the indignant voices of the others.

At the sight of Father Rosario, all the men were suddenly silent.

"What is it, Giorgio?" Father Rosario addressed himself to the standing man.

For a moment Giorgio looked embarrassed and then he mumbled, "It is nothing, Father."

Father Rosario smiled. "You make a great deal of noise over nothing, Giorgio."

We went down a small flight of stone steps to the sand and joined the men. Father Rosario introduced me. Then he turned to Giorgio. "What is the trouble, my son?"

When Giorgio made no answer a young man, wearing an old army battle-dress blouse, looked up at Giorgio and said angrily, "You accuse us, but you are afraid to speak in front of the good Father."

"And of what does Giorgio accuse you, Beppo?" asked Father Rosario.

"Not me alone, Father," answered Beppo, "but also Mario, Giuseppe, and Carlo." He nodded to the others. Mario was a young man, lean and pale-looking; Giuseppe was much older, fat and bald, with a sleepy grin on his face; and Carlo was a thickset, muscular man of nearly sixty with a greying moustache. They sat there, the four of them, cross-legged and barefooted, working at their nets.

"But of what are you accused?" Father Rosario asked gently.

"Of stealing my watch!" Giorgio suddenly exploded. "It is the gold watch, Father, with the fifteen rubies which I had from my father and he from his father and before that—"

"The good Father knows the watch. You wear it across your chest like a great sun every time you go to Mass," said Carlo. "But no longer, for it is stolen and the thief sits here!"

Father Rosario lowered himself to the gunwale of a boat and cocked his head at Giorgio. "I know the watch, Giorgio.

It is very beautiful. But, my son, what makes you think the thief is one of your friends?"

"It is not a thing I say easily, Father. But the truth is the truth. Last night my four friends came to eat and drink at my house. We sat in the little garden and the watch was in the house, in the case on the shelf above my bed, where it always is, and during the evening each of my friends went into the house for one reason and another. The whole evening there was no one else there, and when they left and I went to bed, the watch was gone.

"It is a great loss to me, Father. Not for the value of the watch, though it is entirely of gold and rubies, not for its usefulness, since it does not go; but for its sentimental worth, Father. It has been in my family so long, being given to me by my father who had it from his father and before that—"

Father Rosario raised a thin hand and interrupted him. "It is a possession no man would wish to lose, Giorgio, and it shall be returned to you."

At this I saw the four men look up, the work of their hands stilled momentarily. Father Rosario settled himself more comfortably on the boat's gunwale and his long dark face no longer smiled. He looked around at the men, his eyes travelling from one to the other, and one by one they turned their gaze from him as though in his searching eyes there was a power that made them uncomfortable.

Then slowly he began to speak. "There have, my children, for a long time now been many such petty thefts in our community. You must know of them as I do. It is not a good thing to have amongst us for it turns friend against friend. If among four men there is a thief, then his guilt touches the three innocent men. However, these thefts which we have had here arise not so much from evil or a desire for gain as from vanity or a desire for excitement. Giorgio, if your watch were returned, would you be content never to know the name of the thief?"

Giorgio hesitated for a while, then he said, "If the watch is returned I shall be happy."

"Then it shall be."

"But how can this be, Father?" asked Giuseppe.

"Because, Giuseppe, I know who the thief is." Father Rosario paused and I could sense the surprise and tension amongst the men. Not a man there doubted his word. Father Rosario went on: "He shall return the watch, and later I shall speak to him in private and he will never steal again."

"But if he hands over the watch now, Father, we shall know him," said Giorgio.

"No. It shall be done this way, Giorgio. Beginning with Carlo, each man—Giuseppe, Mario, and Beppo—shall take it in turns to leave us. They shall go across the square and up to your house. Each man shall be given five minutes and then shall return. The thief will put the watch back and you will never know who it is. But I shall know, and he shall answer to me."

I could see how much respect and simple wonder there was in

them for Father Rosario. None of them doubted that he knew already who had the watch, and the thief himself must have felt very uncomfortable at the prospect of his coming interview with Father Rosario.

Carlo, the old man with the moustache, was the first to go. While he was gone we sat and talked and Father Rosario arranged for Giorgio to take me out in his boat. After Carlo's return, Giuseppe went. He came back grinning. Mario and Beppo took their turns.

As Beppo came down the steps Father Rosario rose. "And now, Giorgio, go and get your watch." Father Rosario sent the fisherman off. He was back very quickly, panting and beaming and holding the gold watch.

"It is a miracle, Father!" he cried.

"No, my son, it is not a miracle," Father Rosario said gently. And now think no more of it. These are your friends and will remain your friends. However, there is one man among you who will come to me this evening and we shall talk. Let him not fail to come for then I shall go to him and make his shame public."

We walked away along the sands.

"And who was the thief?" I asked after a while.

Father Rosario smiled. "You do not live amongst us so I shall tell you. It is Giuseppe. He is fat and full of life and very easily bored. During the war he had the finest partisan record of all. He steals not from evil but from a desire to take risks. I shall talk to him about it and he will do it no more."

"And you knew this from the start?"

"No. Only when all the men had returned. Put yourself in their place, my son. What would you have done if you had been one of them, and innocent, and I had sent you to Giorgio's house?"

"I'd have gone across the square, round the corner, waited my five minutes, and come back. Why walk up the hill to a house if I had nothing to replace?"

"Exactly. And that is what they all did—except Giuseppe."

"But how do you know Giuseppe went up to the house?"

"All the men were barefooted. To reach Giorgio's house you have to cross the stepping-stones which are flooded. When Giuseppe returned, his feet were washed free of sand

and his ankles were still wet. The others still had dry, sandy feet."

Father Rosario turned his head towards me and his dark eyes were warm, smiling. "This evening Giuseppe will come to me, and we shall talk together over a glass of wine, and there will be no more thefts."

Fighting Cockerel

I mind the day I first went as a lodger in Barney Doran's house. I wasn't more than a stripling, though I was big for my age and, in those days, I felt I had the world by the tail and was twisting it hard. Barney looks at me and he says, "It's a dirty, unwholesome job ye've got workin' on a newspaper, but I'll take ye in — for your morals will not have been corrupted yet. What'll ye go stripped? About a hundred and thirty pounds, devil a bit more or I'm no judge?"

I might have been a bit puzzled if the lads at the paper had not told me about the old man. In a life which had been full of its fair share of devilry, excitement and decent hard work — though Barney never professed any overdue liking for this last — the old man had been a boxer. And a good one, too, though he was now past it by about twenty years.

"You're right there," I says, "a hundred and twenty-eight."

"Sure, and wasn't I the same at your age."

He looks at me hard and for the moment there was no twinkle at the back of his hard blue eyes. "Do ye think we was fair beat at the Boyne?"

Barney was no Orangeman, and that again was one of the reasons they'd sent me along to him. "You needn't worry over the colours I'll wear on the Twelfth of July," I says, and with that the interviewing was done and Barney set me down with a glass on a chair outside the window and we sat and talked and he told me a lot about himself. A rare, fine talker he was, with just enough imagination to keep a story going without giving anyone cause to name him a liar. Then, just as we were thinking of going in, he says,

"It's an important question I'll ask ye now, so you'll not be saying Barney Doran had ye here under false pretences. Are ye a good sleeper?"

"I never had any trouble," I says.

"Then ye're a lucky man," says Barney, "and I'm hopin' your luck keeps runnin'. I sleep bad meself. Not a decent night's sleep I've known in a long time."

"And why would that be?" I asks him.

"Come with me and I'll show ye the cause av it all," he says, and with that he rises and we go to the bottom of the garden. On the other side of the fence was a strip of land used as a fowl-yard which belonged to Barney's neighbour, Michael Taafe. In the yard were a few white hens and, sitting on top of a box, as fine a cockerel as ever I'd seen.

"There he is," says Barney. "Yon brawlin' braggart murders me sleep ivery mornin'."

Just then the bird begins to crow. It was the evening performance and never did I hear such a noise. The creature seemed fair demented with pride and vigour. It threw back its head and crowed and crowed until it was a wonder it didn't break a blood vessel. Man, it was so fantastic I had to laugh. Sure, and at the same time I couldn't help admiring the bird. It was one of the most beautiful I'd ever seen, with a tawny mantle that fell from its shoulders in a rich, warm gold; its tail feathers had the arch and sweep of an emperor's plumes, green and blue and afire with sheen, and the red of its wattles and the yellow of its legs were as bright as new paint.

"It's a useless devil," says Barney. "You'll hear him at five ivery mornin', tellin' the world what a fine fellow he is. Would ye credit now that such a small body could give out that amount av noise, and all for the admiration of its own useless self? One mornin' I'll take me gun to it, and that'll be the end!"

As Barney was saying this, there comes down to the bottom of the next garden his neighbour, Michael Taafe. Taafe was as old as Barney, but taller, wirier and with not enough meat on his bones to keep his clothes company.

"If iver ye harm that bird, Barney Doran," he says, "I'll have the law on ye."

"Will ye then?" answers Barney. "Maybe ye think ither people is as scared of the law as ye've reason to be?"

They passed a few compliments to one another, and if it hadn't been for Taafe's wife calling to him to come in for supper I'd not have been surprised to see them over the fence at one another.

Later, I learned that Barney and Taafe had been on similar terms for many years. Apart from their political persuasions which, of course, made the whole thing reasonable and entirely natural — Barney being a Nationalist and Taafe an Orangeman — there was also the matter of a small piece of land which Barney owned that lay over the other side of a small stream which bordered Taafe's fowl-yard. Taafe wanted to buy the land and Barney had no intention of selling it at any price, though devil a use did he put the land to himself.

"You should make a complaint to the police," I says one day after I'd been there for some time, for I could see that with an old man like Barney the loss of his sleep was doing him no good.

"I'll make no complaint," says Barney. "But one mornin' that bird will go too far and I'll take me gun to it."

He was always saying he would shoot the bird, but I knew he never would. He was at heart a good-natured man, not the kind to blow an innocent bird into eternity. But each morning, when the cockerel would begin his blathering, Barney would turn in his bed in the room next to mine and there would be a muttering, and then the window would go up with a bang and Barney would lean out in his nightshirt and curse it with a fluency which was an education in itself to a young man like myself just entering the newspaper trade.

Then, after I'd been there about three months, the whole thing came to a head. One morning in July the bird woke me with its crowing and I heard the bang of Barney's window.

"Hush your bawlin', ye painted heathen!" he shouts. "Do ye want me to come and silence ye?"

But the bird only answers him with a clamour fit to wake the dead.

"Ye roarin' braggart" — shouts Barney, — "have ye no respect or decency in your carcase?"

The bird let fly another screech that set the echoes ringing between the houses and I heard Barney shout some more. Then his window went down with a bang the way it was a wonder the glass stood up to it. After a bit I thought I heard Barney downstairs. I lay listening, wondering what the old man was up to. Suddenly there was an awful rattle of echoes against the house as someone fired a shotgun.

Even as I jumped out of bed I said to myself, "Barney, you've done the wrong thing." When I looked out of the window there was Barney at the bottom of the garden, just climbing over the fence into the fowl-yard, and in his hand he carried a smoking shot gun. I pulled on some clothes and ran down. I got into the fowl-yard just as Michael Taafe came tearing through, angry and half-asleep, with his nightshirt tucked into his trousers and his braces trailing behind him like a forked tail.

Barney was standing in the yard holding the shotgun in the crook of his arm, and he had the cockerel held against his breast with his free hand. The bird seemed half-dead, with its eyes lidding over, and the blood was coming from a bad wound in its neck.

"Ye murderin' villain!" screams Michael Taafe. "You shot me bird! I'll have the law on ye for this! You dirty assassin — I've a mind to teach you some decent behaviour meself!"

"Hold your noise, you stupid ould woman," says Barney, " 'Twas you was the instigator av the whole trouble. Do ye want to provoke me?"

Taafe's braces flopped about in the dust as he danced up and down.

"You needn't think you'll come out av this so aisily … Give me the bird!"

"Ye'll not get the bird," says Barney. "If any bird deserved to be shot this one did. If ye're takin' the law av me," says Barney, "ye'll no doubt get your damages. Meantime I'm keepin' the bird, and if you try and take him from me I'll wipe your eye for you and be obliged to wash me hands after …"

Although Barney was fairly calm against Taafe's rage, I'll not say he was being exactly conciliatory, and there was a fair gathering of neighbours around by now, some of them in their nightshirts and some in more decent modes of dress, but all taking a great personal interest in the affair. There were those who felt like Barney — the bird had been a plague to them. But there were others who were for Taafe, because as is natural a man must follow his political feelings regardless of the right or wrong of his cause.

When Barney offered to wipe Taafe's eye, Taafe — with no lack of spirit — says, "And I'd like to see the man who could now. It'll certainly not be you on this day."

And that did it, of course, for we all suddenly remembered what the day was. Sure, it was the Twelfth of July, and even without the bird it would have been fair reason for the larrikins that ensued.

Barney dropped the bird and the gun and went into Taafe like a mole tunnelling a potato patch, and when a neighbour — it was Con McGra — tried to part them he got a swipe on the head from Taafe that knocked him into the chicken hut. Seeing that Barney had McGra with him, it was the proper duty of Big Pete Armstrong to join in to make things even for Taafe. And when Big Pete was in, Danny the Pump joins in for Barney. After a little while, what with one joining in and then another, and no chance of ever getting the odds evened up, it was each man for himself and an occasional woman hanging about the outskirts to bang you over the head with a bat of wood or a garden paling just to keep you in the tight in case you had a mind to up and sneak away before the thing was properly settled — which, in fairness to both sides, I must say was an idea that never once crossed the minds of any of us.

The only complaint I heard afterwards was that the rising dust from the bare earth made it hard to settle who was for or against you, so that there were quite a few that found themselves pitched into the small brook at the edge of the yard by good friends who would never have raised a hand against them if they could have seen properly.

I finished in the brook, but I had the satisfaction of sending one or two there first to establish its fitness for myself, and both Barney and Taafe came in with me. It was while we were getting our wind and thinking of coming out that Father Gorrian arrives and stops the fight. He said some hard words, and there was no arguing with him for his judgment was that on the civil side Barney was in the wrong, though on the religious side he was in the right since a man has a duty to fight for his religion. But that is as it may be. Barney and I went back to the house, and Barney took the bird and his gun with him.

Taafe went back to his house and that day started legal proceedings against Barney for the loss of the bird and also for assault and battery.

"I should av kept me temper, both wi' the bird and wi' Taafe," says Barney inside the house. "Not that I regret anything. No, 'twas as decent a fight, considerin' the day, as a man could ask for."

With that he starts to fuss over the bird. He spent a great deal of time for the next two days over the cockerel, and gradually he got him back to health. It was a miracle of patience how he did it, but done it was, and it seemed to me he wanted to do it as a sort of recompense, for it was not like Barney to shoot at a defenceless bird in that way.

Taafe, of course, brought a charge and the affair became the talk of the town. You see, it wasn't only a question of the bird. It was a question of one faction against another, and when Barney was brought up before the magistrates the place was crowded and Major Dundas had to threaten to clear the place unless people behaved themselves. He was a good man, the major, and although of the same political persuasion as Barney he indulged in no prejudice which any man, in the circumstances, could call unreasonable.

"Ye've heard all the evidence, Barney," he says, "and while I'm not taking into account the political differences involved, for this is no place for them, I'm a little surprised at you. If it had been anyone else but a good Irishman like yourself," and with that he gives a glance towards that part of the court which was packed with Michael Taafe's men, "I could have understood it. But ye're not the kind of man to take a shot at a sitting bird. Why on earth did ye not come and make a complaint in the proper way?"

"Well, your honour," says Barney, "he was disturbin' me sleep and I could stand it no longer. Your honour knows, 'tis a patient man I am, and for months I've stood the yammerin' av that orange-backed, crowin' Billy —"

"Just refer to it as the bird," says the Major with a pleased twist to his face. "There's some in this court would think your reference of 'crowin' Billy' had something to do with the good King William whose memory is evergreen in our loyal hearts."

"Sure, your honour," says Barney. "Well, I'd sworn I'd not be forced to law by this … creature. But that mornin' me temper took the upper hand of me. It's sleep that is a precious thing when ye've reached my age, your honour — as I'm prayin' ye'll live long enough to know for yourself one of these days."

"You shouldn't have shot him, Barney," says the Major. "Ye did wrong."

"I'm not denyin' it," says Barney. "Live and let live. But there it is, your honour. As for the fight afterwards, well — as Father Gorrian has said — there was provocation on both sides, and maybe a deal more on one than the ither —"

"Quite, quite," says the Major, and then after a bit more talk the upshot was that Barney was fined five pounds damages which he paid into the court there and then.

When he came out I was with him, and Michael Taafe comes up.

"Barney Doran," he says, "I'd like me bird back. I understand he's in your house and well recovered."

But Barney shakes his head. "Ye've had your five pounds, Taafe. I'm keepin' the bird," and then he added, sounding a bit embarrassed, "— and if ye don't think that's fair enough, I'll let ye buy that piece of land ye've wanted all along."

So Barney kept the cock and sold his land. He kept the bird in a little run he made in the garden and fetched it a couple of hens for company, but it never crowed again. The injury to its neck had finished its crowing, and all it could do was to give a few clucks now and again. Barney used to sit on a chair watching it. It was very strange how attached he was to the creature now.

Then one day he says, "Ye're wonderin' why I'm so fond av that bird? Ye can't understand it, can ye?"

"Well," says I, "it's just that I can't put the two things comfortably together — you, shooting the bird, and then being so affectionate towards it."

"Faith," says Barney, "seein' that it's real fond av ye I am, I'll tell ye now. But if iver ye breathe a word of it to anyone in this town, I'll wipe your eye for ye."

"I'll not risk that," I says. "What is it now?"

"Well," says Barney, "I was after the blood av that cockerel that mornin'. 'Tis that what counts. I meant murder. That's why I never denied it to the Major — for ye must know that it isn't doin' the deed that makes a man guilty, it's decidin' to do it.

"No. I went down to the empty braggart that mornin' to kill him, but when I got there the crowin' had stopped — and for good reason. There was a weasel in the yard, a long, slim devil of a beast come in after the young birds. There they was, all cooped up in a corner like frightened women folk, and our friend here was havin' a rare set-to with the weasel. Man, he showed me then he wasn't any empty braggart and me heart warmed to him. There he was, jumpin' and leapin', and them wicked spurs going right, left, right, left, as neat and clever as any boxer. But the weasel was no fool, either. He got on to the bird's neck and drew blood bad, but the cockerel threw him off and kept going for his eyes.

"That ould bird knew how to fight, and there was me standin' there that had had him marked for an empty, crowin' rascal for months. Man, the way that bird fought, he had a right to crow. In the end he had the weasel blinded and the beast ran round in circles trying to get out of the yard. That's when I fired. I didn't want the weasel to be away blinded, to die like a miserable sinner in a hole. I finished him wi' a shot and he fell into the brook yonder. Then you all came tearin' down on me ..."

"But Barney," says I, "why did you not tell us?"

"What was there to tell ye? I meant to kill the bird. I would have done it but for that weasel, and then I would have had his blood on me hands. No, as one fighter to another, I was glad to pay the five pounds for him."

Fill the Night with Murder

BARTEO Mondoni was lying flat on the cushions in the stern of the launch. His hands folded behind his head, he was staring up into the sun-burnished sky. A few pigeons from the Piazza San Marco flew across the patch of blue. The air was full o£ the chatter of people moving up and down the waterfront, the cries of hawkers, and the shouts of gondoliers touting for customers.

Humming a little tune to himself, Barteo was inwardly cursing Venice, the people in it, and his own bad luck. Somehow, within the next ten days, he had to find 100,000 lire. If he had any sense, he told himself, he would find it in the same way as he had long ago found enough money to make the step from gondolier to launch proprietor.

Two tourists looked down into the boat and Barteo closed his eyes, pretending to be asleep. He was hired for the afternoon anyway, as he had been every afternoon that week. He lay there, a plump man of forty in a blue shirt and white trousers, his square, browned face topped with black curls. In that moment he decided to do it.

"Barteo!" It was a woman's voice calling from the quay.

Barteo slid off his seat quickly and stood up. A smile cracked his face and his strong white teeth flashed. What a beautiful sight! She stood there in a white silk dress, a red belt about the middle and a touch of red scarf at her throat, and the wind from the water took the lovely sweep of her fair hair and gave it life. Whoever Signor Lampson was, thought Barteo, he was a lucky man to have such a wife—and rich. The rings on her fingers would have paid off the debt on Barteo's launch and kept him and his wife, Maria, for years.

"Signora Lampson," he called cheerfully. "*Ben venuto* ...." He reached up and helped her into the launch as though she were a princess.

"Barteo," she greeted him. "Always laughing, always gay! This afternoon I have brought a friend and you must sing some of my favourite songs for him."

As she stepped by him, Barteo saw that a man was standing on the quay waiting to come aboard. Barteo gave the man a little bow and then helped him in. At once he disliked him.

This man, he knew at once, wasn't her husband. She had shown him a photograph of her husband, a large, bulky-shouldered man, well into his fifties. "He goes bald, Barteo," she had said, laughing. "That is because he works so hard to make money for me to spend ..." No, this man wasn't her husband. He was young and expensive-looking—the kind Barteo saw around Harry's bar—with wide shoulders that fell away to slim hips and a dark, hard-cut face with large, cold eyes. The kind of eyes that remained without expression even when he smiled.

Barteo's afternoon was spoiled. He took them into the shallow lagoons toward Burano. Venice fell back on the skyline in a delicate frieze of towers and domes. He drove fast because Signora Lampson insisted on it, and he sang for them, but his heart wasn't in it, for all the time he could see the two of them sitting in the stern.

Giasone—for he had heard her call him that—could have dropped dead and the launch owner would have been unmoved. Barteo decided that if he had to go back to his old pickpocket ways of finding money he would start with Giasone.

And he did … Two hours later as he helped the pair out of the launch at San Marco, he expertly picked Giasone's wallet from the man's inside pocket! He watched them go off, arm in arm. Then, squatting down by the engine, he opened the wallet; it contained a few letters, a driving license, and 50,000 lire. It was a lucky first haul. In a week if such luck held he would have his 100,000 lire. Giasone wouldn't miss his wallet for some time. By then anyone might have taken it. All Barteo had to do was to throw the empty wallet overboard on his way home. He began to straighten up.

As he did so someone jumped into the launch behind him. He turned quickly to find himself facing Giasone. On the quay was Signora Lampson. Giasone just stared at him with his hard, still eyes. Then he reached back and took Signora Lampson's hand and helped her in.

"Start up and go out," said Giasone curtly.

Barteo looked at Signora Lampson, She was beautiful and poised, but for the first time he saw a hint of ruthlessness about her unsmiling mouth.

"Do as he says, Barteo." There was no warmth in her voice.

Barteo took them out and down toward the Lido and then at a sign from Giasone he shut off the engine.

Giasone broke the silence. "You were unlucky, Barteo: A few moments after we left you I wanted to show Signora Lampson a letter from my wallet. Very unlucky."

Barteo took the wallet from his pocket. "Here it is, *signor*. I ask your forgiveness."

Giasone shook his head. "Keep it. You can tell your story to the police."

"The police? But, *signor*, is it necessary?" Barteo turned toward Signora Lampson. "*Signora*, cannot the whole thing be forgotten?"

"Why should it be?"

Fear stirred in Barteo. "But you do not understand, *signora*. Years ago, when I was a gondolier, I served several sentences for theft. If you take me to the police now, I shall get the maximum sentence … and I have been straight for years and years. It will kill my wife. You understand, she has not been well. I have had to spend money on doctors for her and so the instalments on this boat have fallen behind. Otherwise, I would not have done this … Oh, *signora*, please understand … I had to find the money by the end of the month."

Giasone looked at Signora Lampson. She turned to Barteo

"Barteo," she said gently, and there was a smile on her face now. "How much do you need to pay off your debt?"

"A hundred thousand lire, *signora*."

"We could show you a way of earning that, a way out of your troubles, Barteo—if you would help us. We could forget all about the police."

"*Signora*, I will do anything," said Barteo eagerly.

Giasone chuckled and the sound was like pebbles being washed together by the sea. "It is a little thing, Barteo. But do not try to make fools of us. I have a quick temper. On a dark night a man might find himself in a canal."

"What is it?" asked Barteo.

"Tomorrow Signora Lampson's husband arrives in Venice. You are a man of the world, you will understand that Signora Lampson is no longer interested in her husband, only in his money. It would be convenient if he had an accident. Then I could marry the *signora* … and we should be so happy. You, too, Barteo. We should all be happy."

Barteo knew they were in earnest. They would turn him over to the police as ruthlessly as they planned murder.

"Tomorrow evening," went on Giasone, "you will take the three of us out to Torcello. Signor Lampson wants us to dine at the Locanda Ristorante. He has a passion for the pressed duck they serve there. On the way back you will stop and sing us some songs. Then, unfortunately, Signor Lampson—who will have had too much to drink—will fall overboard. Although we go round and round looking for him he is not picked up. Alas, he cannot swim … So simple, so natural."

"But I can't. That would be—"

"An accident," said Giasone.

"I won't do it!" Barteo shouted.

"So? Then let us go to the police now. *Avanti*!"

But Barteo didn't move. He was in their hands and he knew it. He sat there for a long while and they waited, and in the end he said almost inaudibly, "Very well. I will do it."

"You are sensible, Barteo," said Signora Lampson.

That night Barteo lay in bed by his sleeping wife and tried to find a way out. But he could see none. If he knew where Signor Lampson lived or where he would be staying in Venice, he could tell him the whole story. The man might well pay him the 100,000 lire he needed for the warning and use his influence with the police to quash any charge of theft. But he had no way of finding Signor Lampson. And if he went to the police—who had no love for him anyway—

Giasone would deny everything, and he would never get the money he wanted, his boat would be lost and later the blow would come from the darkness.

He spent the next day in misery, sitting in his boat well out in the lagoon, searching for some solution. But at 8:30 he was waiting in his launch for his party to arrive.

"Barteo!"

She was standing on the quay, gay and smiling, her body sheathed in a gold dress, the sparkle of jewels about her neck and arms, a fur across the lovely bare shoulders. So beautiful, he thought, and so evil. With her, in evening dress, was Giasone and another man—Signor Lampson, a big hulking figure with a ponderous, humorous face.

Barteo went forward and helped them all in. They went out across the waters to Torcello, a half hour away. Behind him Barteo could hear them laughing and joking, and the sound made him feel sick. Once Giasone came forward to him and he felt the hard pressure of a gun in his side.

"*Va bene*, Barteo?" The harsh whisper was close to his ear.

He nodded.

He switched the headlight on as they ran into the narrow canal that led up to the landing stage for the Locanda restaurant. He helped them all out and then sat there, watching them as they went up the little stretch of rough road to the Locanda.

It was nearly three hours, close to midnight, when he heard them coming back. As he helped the man aboard, Signor Lampson said, "My wife tells me you're a good singer, Barteo. You must give us some songs on the way back." His breath smelled of wine and he had a couple of bottles under his arm. "Barteo shall fill the night with song!" called Signora Lampson, and she put her arm about her husband's shoulder and rubbed her cheek against his. Barteo turned away, unable to watch, and started the engine.

From that moment Barteo lived in a black dream full of anxiety. When the lights of Venice were still distant on the steely face of the lagoon waters, he stopped the launch and switched off the headlights.

"Song and wine!" shouted Giasone. Barteo sang, and the bottle went round. Signor Lampson, full of wine and good spirits; joined in. Then, after about ten minutes, it happened. Signor Lampson stood up, announcing that he would sing a song. His great bulk swayed unsteadily. Barteo saw Giasone rise and throw himself against the man. There was a shout, a moment of struggle, and then Signor Lampson was overboard. Giasone jumped forward to Barteo, the automatic in his hand.

"*Avanti! Presto!*"

Barteo started the engine and with a roar the launch moved away into the darkness toward Venice. Not for five minutes would Giasone allow Barteo to put the headlights on.

Barteo sat with Signora Lampson and Giasone in a room on the second floor of the Questura. Outside ran the Rio dei Greci where the launch was moored. Barteo listened to Giasone telling the story of the accident. Signor Lampson had been a little drunk … It was so unfortunate … They had searched frantically … Alas, he could not swim.

Signora Lampson was the picture of a woman numbed with shock. The police captain rested his chin in his hands and nodded now and again. When Giasone had finished, the captain rose and said, "We will send a police launch out to make another search." He nodded at Barteo. "Come, you can take them to the place." Barteo followed him out of the room and, as. he walked, he could feel the stiff crackle of notes from the 100,000 lire which Giasone had paid him on the way back.

When the two were gone Signora Lampson and Giasone sat and waited. They waited so long that Signora Lampson said finally, anxiety moving into her voice, "Why are they so long? Why do they leave us here?"

Giasone shrugged. "You know the police ... They have no respect for people's feelings." But there was an edge of doubt in his own voice and he got up, glancing at his watch. It was too long. Over an hour. He began to move toward the door, to find someone and make a protest.

But as he neared the door there was the sound of voices from outside and it swung open. Giasone stepped back and Signora Lampson rose and calve to his side.

Into the room came the police captain and Barteo. Behind them, wrapped in blankets, was the bulky figure of Signor Lampson.

"*Caro!*" cried Signora Lampson, all her woman's quickness coming to her aid.

The police captain said, "Signora Lampson and you, Signor, are under arrest for the attempted murder of Signor Lampson."

Giasone's hand dropped swiftly to his pocket and he turned toward Barteo. "You dirty little—"

Signor Lampson, astonishingly quick for so big a man, jumped forward and took Giasone by the wrist, twisting it vigorously. The automatic dropped to the floor. Signor Lampson picked it up.

"Barteo is my friend," he said. "My very good friend. But for him—and I shall repay him handsomely—I should indeed be floating in the lagoon." There was a grim smile of satisfaction on his face as he looked from Giasone to his wife. "When I stepped aboard Barteo's launch in Venice this evening, he stole my wallet. On the way over he slipped a letter into it. At Torcello, as he helped me ashore, he replaced my wallet. He is an expert pickpocket, but no murderer. When I took out my wallet to pay the bill at the restaurant I found the letter. I read it in front of you, but you were too busy looking into one another's eyes to notice. Love is blind ..."

He laughed. "Barteo explained everything in the letter. He said he would stop the launch in a part of the lagoon where—although far from land—the water was only two feet deep, so I could stand safely waiting for the police to arrive ..." He reached out and patted Barteo on the shoulder, but Barteo was looking at Signora Lampson. So beautiful in her golden gown ... so beautiful ...

Sanctuary for the General

Major-General Sir Henry Braithwaite, K.B.E., C.B., D.S.O., M.C., known to his friends as Galloper, was having breakfast. *The Times* was propped against the coffee pot, and he was spreading marmalade on his toast with a thin-bladed pygmy hunting-knife which had come from the Ituri forests of the Congo. The May morning sunshine streamed through the mullioned windows of the breakfast-room of Lambertill Hall and there was a lingering aroma of kippers in the air. Kippers were Sir Henry's favourite breakfast food, and the two he had just finished were the first he had had in eighteen months.

The General was a fine, intimidating figure of a man. His fair hair was now thin and whitening, his blue eyes clear and frank against a suntanned complexion, and his beaked Roman nose presided over a fierce cavalry moustache. As the chairman of a committee, a justice of the peace, or a judge at a horse show, the General stood no nonsense from anyone. In fact, it would have been difficult for the General to remember the last time he had ever stood any nonsense from anyone in any walk of life. He snorted now at a piece of nonsense in the third leader and threw the paper to the floor just as his man, Murch, came into the room. Murch — once Trooper Murch — was the only indoor servant the General could afford.

"Timms, sir, is outside, sir, waiting to see you," said Murch.

"Timms? What does he want? I said I'd walk round with him this afternoon."

"He said something about the bulldozer, sir."

"The bulldozer? What are you talking about, Murch?"

"The bulldozer, sir."

"I heard you the first time. But what bulldozer?"

"I wouldn't know, sir. I don't meddle with the outside things. I've enough to do in here, sir."

The General cocked an eye at Murch, but wisely did not pursue this aspect of the conversation. Murch, gloomy, sardonic, but utterly faithful to the General, had been agitating in his own peculiarly devious way for two years to get the General to buy him a washing-up machine. Actually, the General might have been able, with a little pinching here and there, to run to a washing-up machine. But the real snag was that there was no electricity at Lambertill Hall.

"Excellent kippers, Murch. Excellent. If it's possible, your touch has improved while I've been away."

The General got up and went out, a tall well-built figure in shooting-jacket and breeches. Timms was waiting for him in the driveway, a shotgun crooked under his arm. Timms — once Trooper Timms — was the outside man, the gardener and game-keeper of two-hundred-odd acres — all that was now left of the Lambertill estate, the rest having long been sold to pay taxes.

These two hundred acres of wild heath, woodland, and marsh, running down to the North Sea, the General had turned into a bird sanctuary. Ornithology was the passion of the General's life. The only shooting that was ever done on the Lambertill Estate was of vermin, like rats and squirrels, that plagued the nesting birds. After a lifetime of warfare in various parts of the globe the General had become, in his own way, a man of peace.

"Morning, Timms. What the devil's all this about a bulldozer?"

"Morning, General. It's the bulldozer for the new road, sir. Thought you'd like to know they're making a start."

"Bulldozer? What road?"

"The new road, sir. Coming in by the quarry copse they are, off the Lamindon road."

"What the devil is this?" The General's blue eyes glinted fiercely. "My gold-crested wrens nest every year in the pines down there. Come on, man — let's get to the bottom of this. New road! Has someone gone mad while I've been away?"

The General strode off, followed by Timms.

Half a mile from the Hall, where the country road to the small town of Lamindon bordered the estate, there was a clump of pines at the side of an old quarry. As they approached, the General saw that a man was busy pulling up a length of chestnut paling while another man sat in the driving-seat of a bulldozer waiting to move in. Somebody, the General noticed in fury, had stuck a row of surveyor's red-and-white stakes across the ground running from the quarry into the estate.

Seeing the man busy on his chestnut paling, the General took the gun from Timms and fired a couple of shots into the air, well above the man's head. The man sat back, surprised, into the ditch and was still sitting there when the General arrived.

"What the devil do you two think you're doing?" roared the General, and Timms, hearing the thunder in his voice, was taken back to his days in tanks when the General had commanded an Armoured Division.

The man pulled himself from the ditch and said petulantly, "You shot at me!"

"Don't talk damned nonsense, man! I shot over you. What's going on here?"

The man on the bulldozer took a cigarette from his mouth and said amiably, "The new road, General. Cuts right across to Lambertill beach and then on to Sandfields. We've just got to make an entrance for the lorries and other stuff to get in. Nice to see you back, General."

For a moment the General looked in silence from one man to the other. Like a good tactician he made a quick appreciation of the situation, and arrived at two conclusions: one, nobody was taking down his fence and driving a bulldozer through his land and, two, this outrage had to be tackled at source.

He snorted and said commandingly, "Timms, stay here. If either of them lays a hand on that fence or tries to drive that machine in — shoot."

"Yes, sir."

"I'll go and find out about this."

The amiable man on the bulldozer nodded. "That's right, General. But it won't do you any good. All signed and sealed, it is."

"Then it will all be unsigned and unsealed, my man!"

The General turned and strode off, fuming. His land, his birds, all to be mucked up with a new road to Lambertill beach and Sandfields when there was already a perfectly good — if longer — road running round the back of the estate!

Half an hour later he drove into Lamindon in his open, vintage Phantom II Rolls-Royce, intent on visiting his solicitor. As he parked his car in front of the Town Hall, a young constable came up to him.

"Sorry, sir — you can't park your car there. New regulation. Reserved for the Mayor and council members."

This was the last straw to the General.

"Listen, young man," he said, "I've been parking my car there for years, and before I had a car I parked my bicycle there, and my grandfather parked his penny-farthing there before me. Give the Mayor my compliments and tell him and the town council to sue me and be damned! Now, don't delay me any longer!"

He strode off to the offices of Wench, Welton, and Barnhill, Solicitors and Commissioners for Oaths, leaving the young constable open-mouthed.

A few minutes later he crashed into Harvey Wench's office. Harvey, a pleasant, competent young man, had served under the General in World War II, and now handled all the General's legal affairs.

"Good morning, General. You're just in time for a glass of sherry."

"I don't want sherry, young feller. I want an explanation. What have you been up to, you nincompoop? What is all this about a new road to Sandfields through my place? A new road — right across one of the finest stretches of country around here. Disturbing my bittern and shrike! What have you been doing while I've been away?"

Harvey waited for the gale to subside and then said patiently, "But, General — I wrote to you about this while you were away. It's part of the new county development scheme for Lambertill beach and Sandfields. The Minister has given his consent — after a public hearing. Surely you remember? You sent me a telegram telling me to go ahead. It only cuts across a corner of your land and you get — I must say this — very handsome compensation."

"I don't care a fig for the compensation. I'm thinking of my bird sanctuary. And what letter? What telegram? I didn't get any letters in the Ituri forest. D'you think there's a postal service in the middle of the Congo? And the only telegram I sent you was about those shares of mine you were fussing over before I left — those property holdings. I changed my mind and wired you before I went up-country — GO THROUGH WITH PROPERTY DEAL MENTIONED BY YOU."

Harvey's face fell. "Oh dear — there's been a ghastly mix-up. I thought your telegram was an answer to my letter."

"I don't care what you or anyone else thought! Just tell the county people to haul off their bulldozers. I'm not selling any more of my land. Anyone who wants to go to Lambertill beach can go round by the old road, or across the estate bridlepath. I've never stopped people coming on my place so long as they behave themselves. Encouraged 'em, in fact. But I'm not having any damn road with cars whizzing about, disturbing the birds. In no time they'll be setting up hot-dog stands and lord knows what. Turning the foreshore into a lido or some damn rot like that. People want a sanctuary as much as the birds — and that's what Lambertill is going to remain. A sanctuary."

Harvey shook his head. "It can't be done, General. The whole thing is signed and sealed. You know what these official bodies are like."

"Have you had the cheque for the sale?"

"No."

"Then that's it. I won't accept it. Just tell them the whole thing is off. Phone the County Surveyor now and tell him to recall that bulldozer. Tell him Timms and I will shoot anyone who tries to come in."

"But, General —"

"No buts. Get cracking." The General turned on his heels and left the room before Harvey could say anything.

He went back to his car, and the young constable on duty, watching him drive off, decided that it might be better not to report the parking offence.

That weekend Harvey carne over to Lambertill Hall to report progress.

"I'm sorry, General," he said. "But there is nothing we can do. They say they're not responsible for the mistake and they must go ahead."

"What?" The General's roar echoed round the library. "Go ahead, must they? We'll see about that!"

Harvey recognised that the General was now in one of his 'Galloper' moods. In other words, when surrounded by the enemy, he was prepared to give his charger its head, draw his sword and, backed by stalwart troopers, cut his way out.

"I'm afraid we're too late," said Harvey nervously. "The Minister has given his authority for this thing, the County Council are all on their toes ready to go, Government grants have been made —"

"And the whole thing has been a mistake. I've never given permission and I never will!" exploded the General.

" There was a public inquiry into the affair. They say that you should have objected then."

"How could I ? Don't be a blithering idiot! I was in Africa and knew nothing. All they have to do is to see that and cancel everything. But not them. They're so tied up in red tape that once a thing has been settled they've no idea how to unsettle it."

"They don't want to, that's why. And anyway, they can always make a compulsory purchase order against you."

"What? Force me to sell my own land? What is this country — a concentration camp? Don't people have any rights to their own property?"

"Not if they stand in the way of beneficial developments."

"Beneficial! What's beneficial about a new road when there's a perfectly adequate old one? What's beneficial about turning a quiet beach into a jam-packed lido? And what about the hundreds of people who take civilised pleasure in walking round the sanctuary watching the birds, eh? And what about the birds, eh? What about them? Are they going to like it? Do you think any self-respecting godwit, Sandwich tern, or spotted flycatcher is going to nest around here if this road goes through?"

"There isn't a thing I can do, General."

The General snorted and fixed himself a whisky and soda. "Harvey, that's just the spineless kind of thing that you would say. Tie a piece of red tape round something and it becomes sacred to you. If a thing is wrong, it's wrong, and they've got to put it right. I'll make them!"

"What can you do?" Harvey asked.

"Fight them! Right the way up to the top. Already I've told the Chairman of the County Council Highways Committee that he will never be invited to dinner here again, and that his fishing syndicate's lease on Lambertill lake will not be renewed next year unless all work is suspended for a month."

"He agreed?"

"He had to. I've got a month's respite. I'm going to London on Monday to see Bunty Haggerty."

"Who's he?"

"Bunty? He used to be a pimple-faced squirt at Charterhouse with me. Used to make him do my Latin and Greek prep for me. Odd blighter — never played games. Always poking round old churches, digging up flint arrowheads. Mad on archaeology. At the moment he happens to be the Right Hon. Bernard Willoughby Haggerty, M.P., member of Her Majesty's Cabinet and Minister of Rural Transport and Civil Aviation. Don't ask me why. He probably thinks a Sopwith Camel was something with four legs, and he's the fool who's given permission for roads to be plastered all over the country in places where people don't want 'em."

And on Monday the General motored to London and went to see the Right Hon. Bernard Willoughby Haggerty.

It was no tender reunion. Bunty, a short, plump, and rather pompous man, was polite — hiding successfully a long-ingrained nervousness of the Galloper's pugnacious manner — but he could offer no balm. The scheme was all settled and must go through.

"Bunty," fumed the General, "I'm warning you that I'm not taking no for an answer. This is going higher. Where's the P.M.? I'll see him."

"The Prime Minister is in Paris. He doesn't get back for, a week. There's nothing you can do, General. Believe me."

"We'll see. How the devil would you like someone driving a road across your ground?"

"If it were in the national interest I should submit gracefully."

"Then you'd be a fool. National interest. That's what they always say when they have no real argument. Right — then I'll go above the P.M."

"I should like to know where."

"Then I'll tell you." And the General mentioned the name of a Very High Royal Person indeed.

For a moment Bunty's face paled. "You know him?"

"As good as. Damn it, I nearly married his wife, didn't I? When I was a subaltern, Poppy and I were very good friends. But she decided in the end to plump for being a Duchess rather than a camp follower to a warrior. Don't blame her."

And to Poppy the General went. The Duchess, no longer the slim, giggling debutante whom the General had once known, was charmed to see him. He sat in her boudoir and they had tea together and talked over old times, and then they were joined by her husband, the Duke, and to the two of them the General put his problem.

"Bird sanctuary, eh?" said the Duke. "No shootin'?"

"No, sir. Only with a camera."

"Dull, what?"

"Of course it isn't," said the Duchess. "It's much harder to get a good picture of a marsh harrier feeding its young than it is to knock down a couple of high-flying pheasants."

"That so? Interestin'."

"You must do something for Galloper," said Poppy.

"True, my love," said the Duke. "But so far as I can see it's birds, peace, and quiet against a new road. Not much argument there. Some like birds and peace and quiet, and just as many like new roads and noisy beaches. I mean, if they wanted to knock down St. Paul's and make a road through, or Nelson's Column, then there'd be something to work on. But I'll try. Going to Paris tomorrow. Could have a word with the P. M."

Two days later the General had a telephone call from the Duchess to say that the Duke's plea had been sympathetically heard by the Prime Minister, but very diplomatically turned down. This was a departmental matter and not of sufficient national importance to warrant interference from him at this late stage.

Many another man would have taken this as final. But not Galloper Braithwaite. He brooded on the matter for a whole day, and then in the evening wandered into the kitchen where Murch was washing up. For some time the General said nothing, but he absently took a dish towel and began to dry the plates. Murch gave him a gloomy look and waited, silently.

After a time the General said, " Murch, how much does one of these washer things cost?"

"About sixty pounds, I think, sir."

"I see."

"There would be the installing of the electricity as well, sir."

"How much?"

"About three hundred pounds, I understand, sir."

"I see."

"Not that I am not content with things as they are, sir. But it is a bit hard on the hands. Always was prone to chapping, sir, as you know. Early morning stables was a nightmare to me sometimes, sir."

"Call it four hundred pounds altogether, eh?" The General grunted. "Well, we might manage it, Murch. We might — if you cooperate."

"Cooperate, sir?"

"In a little scheme. Could be dangerous, though. I mean, it calls for courage and discretion."

"Illegal, sir?" Murch knew the General.

"In a way."

"I'd be delighted, sir. Anything to save my hands, sir."

"Good — then get Timms in here and we'll fix it up."

"Timms, sir?"

"It's an outside as well as an inside job. And I shall need you both to come to London with me the day after tomorrow.

A road across my land, eh? Scaring my birds, mucking the place up for decent folk on the beach — I'll show them!"

Two evenings later, at six o'clock, the General walked into the bar of his club, not far from Claridge's Hotel in Brook Street, and found, as he knew he would, Sir James Knowland, the millionaire proprietor of the *Daily World*, contemplating his sixth whisky of the day.

"Evening, Jimmy."

"Evening, Galloper. Whisky?"

"Thank you."

They drank in silence for a while, and then the General said casually, "Tell me, Jimmy — how much would your paper pay for a real scoop?"

"Depends, Galloper. Real big stuff no limit."

"Indeed. Well, four hundred quid is all a friend of mine wants. First-class story, too. You could just catch the press tonight with it. Absolutely exclusive."

"What is it?"

"Not so fast, Jimmy. First — the money would have to be paid to me, and the whole thing is in strict confidence. After all, the fellow's doing me a great service."

"You sure there is a friend, Galloper? "

"If that's your attitude, I can take this somewhere else."

Sir James Knowland shook his head. "Four hundred to you. Strict confidence. If the story is good."

"Read this."

The General handed over a typewritten sheet to Sir James. Sir James read it, whistled, and broke into a great smile. "No stopping you, is there, Galloper? O. K. Strict confidence. Money in the mail to you tonight. Sorry, I must hurry."

The next morning, at the breakfast tables of those fortunate enough to subscribe to the *Daily World*, the news broke. Within a few hours the wires all over the country and the world were humming with it.

The Right Hon. Bernard Willoughby Haggerty, M.P., Minister of Rural Transport and Civil Aviation, had been kidnapped, changing for dinner at his house.

An anonymous communication received by the editor of the *Daily World* announced that the kidnapper, an admirer of Major-General Sir Henry Braithwaite, and also a passionate ornithologist and campaigner for the preservation of the rural beauties of England, meant to hold on to the Right Hon. Bernard Willoughby Haggerty until the scheme to drive a road through the Lambertill Bird Sanctuary was withdrawn. If the scheme were not withdrawn the Right Hon. Bernard Willoughby Haggerty would never see the light of day again.

The repercussions were many and rapid. The Lambertill road scheme, which had been only of local interest, suddenly became of international interest. The legion of societies for and against planning, for and against new roads, for and against wild life and rural preservation, and so on, went into action with a spate of letters to the press. The manservant of Bunty Haggerty, besieged by reporters, could only say that his master had gone up to change for dinner and had never come down. His black tie was still laid out on the bed, but the rest of his evening clothes had disappeared with him.

Nearer home the exchanges were sharper. Harvey Wench rang the General and told him that he would never get away with it. The General replied, "Don't know what you're talking about. Nothing to do with me. Damned nice of whoever it was."

The Duchess, staying at a nearby country house, telephoned and said, "Galloper, how like you. So dashing! But it won't do any good. Wrap him up and send him back."

The General thanked her for her interest and invited her to dinner the following weekend.

The Chief Constable of the County, prodded from Scotland Yard — they in turn prodded by the Prime Minister — arrived at Lambertill Hall with a search warrant.

"Hope you haven't got this chap around, Galloper. Look bad for you if I turn him up."

The General, who hunted regularly with the Chief Constable, gave him a glass of sherry and told him to have a good look round. The Chief Constable and his men departed without finding any trace of the Right Hon. Bernard Willoughby Haggerty.

And there the matter was. A member of Her Majesty's Cabinet missing, an ultimatum issued, the preliminary work for the road halted, and the General, Murch, and Timms going about their business with cheerful unconcern. Yes, even Murch was cheerful, for the General had written to the local contractors for an estimate for installing electricity in the Hall, and Murch was happily collecting brochures of washing-up machines.

Bunty Haggerty was, of course, at Lambertill. His kidnapping had been a matter of no great difficulty to three seasoned campaigners like the General, Murch, and Timms.

Some half a mile from the Hall there was a large range of dunes, a favourite nesting place for sand martins. Here — during World War II — an anti-aircraft gun had been sited. The gun was now long gone, but there remained an old ammunition store which the gunners had dug into the sandy side of the dune and lined with logs. The stout door to the store was now overgrown with a wilderness of tamarisk and gorse bushes and it would have needed the eyes of a hawk to spot it. Here the General visited Bunty each evening after nightfall, accompanied by Timms carrying food and drink for the beleaguered member of Her Majesty's Cabinet.

The General was sitting with him now, an old cavalry sword resting across his knees in case Bunty tried to escape. Timms had retired. Bunty, in evening dress less a black tie, watching the glint of hurricane lamplight on the sword, was openly nervous, but also pugnacious.

"You'll never get away with this, Galloper. You've really put yourself in the soup."

"Pooh and bah!" said the General. "They'll come round. Every day you stay here, work piles up at your Ministry. They'll have to come round."

"And if they don't?"

"I'll send them first your right ear and then your left. Or the other way round if you prefer it."

"You can't play ducks and drakes with the Government like this. You're mad."

"If the Government can play ducks and drakes with me and my bird sanctuary, I can do the same with them. Trouble with people these days is they won't stand up for their rights against you red-tape-ridden bureaucrats."

The General stood up to go. As he did so, his eye fell on a spade at the far end of the store where the logs holding back the sand had rotted away. Fresh sand lay over the ground. The General cocked an eye at Bunty. "Been digging, I see."

Bunty replied belligerently, "I've a right to try and escape."

"Certainly," said the General. "Duty of every officer when taken prisoner. But you'll never make it that way. Two hundred yards of solid dune. But it's healthy exercise. Good night."

For four days the mystery of the missing Cabinet member obsessed the nation, and for four days various members of the

Government and as many of the War Office — old friends of Galloper's, and all convinced that he was holding Bunty Haggerty somewhere — applied pressure in their different ways to make him see sense.

To all of them the General made substantially the same reply. "If the Lambertill road goes through you'll have to get a new Minister. With thousands of others, I fought for this country in its hour of need. I'm not standing by now to see it desecrated by a lot of bureaucratic morons who don't know how to change their minds. They're the kind who've made the dodo and the Cornish red-legged chough extinct, and wouldn't turn a hair if the golden eagle went the same way. Sanctuary is what we need for birds and men."

But in the end a pressure was brought on the General which he could not resist. When the Duchess came to dinner with him that weekend, the Duke came as well. They ate in the long dining-hall by candlelight, and when the port was served Poppy refused to leave the men.

The Duke sipped his glass, held it up to the candlelight, and with that air of wellbeing which comes from good port only, said, " I'm not sure. Could be a Gould-Campbell, 1927."

"Cockburn, '27," said the General. "Only six dozen left. See me out."

The Duke nodded and then said, " Talkin' of seein' you out … might not be long, head on a block, what, and all that — if you hang on to Bunty Haggerty."

Poppy, smiling graciously at the General, said, "You've got to turn him loose, Galloper."

" 'Fraid so," said the Duke. "Do it now, no repercussions. Whole matter smoothed over. But the P.M. is worried. Government being made to look foolish. Laughin' stock of the world. Bad for international relations, you know."

The General circulated the port, watched the Duke refill his glass, and realised that he was being given an order; and the order was coming from a man who, in the strict military sense, was his commander.

Sadly, thinking of his birds and of the lovely stretch of wild country which so many people enjoyed in peace and quiet, all now to be changed, he said, "Of course, sir."

Poppy, sorry for him, said, "It was a good try, Galloper, my dear. But these are modern times ... people don't understand."

"Better get him now," said the Duke. "I'll talk to him and see he doesn't get any ideas about making trouble. Where is he?"

The General told him, and the Duke and Duchess, since it was a fine evening, decided to walk to the dunes with the General. They found Bunty Haggerty at the back of the store, digging away by the light of two hurricane lamps. For a while he was unaware of their presence.

"Tryin' to escape?" queried the Duke.

The General shook his head. "More for exercise than anything else, sir. Keeps him fit. He's been doing it ever since I put him here. Hey, Bunty!"

The Right Hon. Bernard Willoughby Haggerty turned and, recognising the Duke and Duchess, came forward to be greeted by them. He looked dirty, dishevelled, and exhausted, but there was a curious glint in his eyes.

"Sentence remitted," said the General. "You're free. Come back to the Hall and clean up. Give you a comfortable bed for the night."

"No hard feelings," said the Duke. "Forget and forgive."

"That's an order, of course," said Poppy, winking at the General. "Forget and forgive."

"Forget!" cried Bunty, finding his voice. "I'll never forget my time here as long as I live! The world is going to know about it!"

"Now — come, come!" soothed the Duke.

"No, you come, sir," said Bunty. "This way. Come and look at this."

He started back to the end of the store where he had dug into the wall about ten feet, opening a great space. He held up a hurricane lamp and his eyes shone. "Look — it must be! Archaeologists have been looking for it for years. But always round the present site of Lamindon. But it's been here all the time, five miles away."

Under the lamplight they saw a spread of tessellated pavement, in its centre an intricate blue and green dolphin design surrounded by men and women in ancient clothes. The colours glowed richly under the soft lamplight.

"Roman mosaic," said Poppy. "How lovely!"

"It's the lost Roman city of Laminium!" cried Bunty. "Floor of a villa. There must be others, all hidden under these dunes. A great archaeological treasure. It could be bigger than Verulamium —"

"And you're going to drive a road through the lot," said the General sourly. "New road comes right across these dunes."

"New road!" Bunty almost shrieked. "Vandalism! There's going to be no new road across here! We can't destroy the country's antiquities. I'd be blackballed from the Athenaeum, thrown out of every archaeological society in the country if I allowed it. I'll fight it tooth and nail."

"Absolutely," said the Duke. "Like driving a road through St. Paul's. No one would stand for it."

The General looked at Poppy, and she said quietly, " No road."

"No road," said the General, and he was thinking happily of the splendid stretches of Roman paving which would be brought into the sunlight. Here, in the heart of his sanctuary, people would be able to enjoy the beauties of a past civilisation and the pleasures of bird wild-life. There would be some disturbance while the old villas were being uncovered, but that would soon pass. He would keep an eye on things … A car park down on the Lamindon road and then a quiet walk along the bridlepath to ancient Laminium …

"Don't just stand there," said the Duke to the General, cutting in on his reverie. "Go and get a couple more spades. I want to see what the rest of the floor looks like."

"Yes, sir," said the General.

"And bring the rest of that Cockburn 1927 with you. Going to be thirsty work. Haggerty and I will be needing it."

Vintage Vendetta

The auctioneer let the buzz of excitement around the room subside. Then, in a fat, satisfied voice, he said, "One thousand pounds I am offered. One thousand pounds, ladies and gentlemen. Any advance on one thousand pounds?"

He looked across m the direction of Professor Patrick Walter Fitzharris, M.Sc., F.I.M., F.R.Ae.S., now retired, but at one time Professor of Industrial Metallurgy at Midland University, member of the Council of United Kingdom Metals Association, and author of *Principles of Foundry Metallurgy*, which, while not as exciting as *Gone with the Wind*, in the last twenty years had sold almost as many copies throughout the world. The Professor glared back at the auctioneer, all his Irish blood stirred up.

The Professor was a short, wiry, jockey-sized man of about sixty, grey-haired, and with bright blue eyes now sparkling with frustration. At his side sat Lydia Annette Fitzharris, his daughter, blonde, with softer blue eyes than her father, a willowy figure in tweeds, the air about her faintly touched with the fragrance of Miss Dior. She put a hand on his arm and said, "Control yourself, Daddy — you can't afford it."

"Control myself, is it," growled the Professor, his anger emphasising his native brogue. "I want it and I'm going to have it. What would a man be if he only bought the things he could afford?"

"Solvent," said Lydia crisply.

"Then it's no way to live," said the Professor.

"One thousand pounds — for the first time," began the auctioneer. "One thousand pounds — for the second time —"

"Guineas!" barked the Professor.

Lydia raised her eyes to heaven and gave up.

"Thank you, Professor," said the auctioneer, smiling, and then announced to the company, "One thousand guineas I am offered. One thousand guineas ..." He went off into his patter and his head was now turned to a distant part of the saleroom.

While he did so, the Professor said in a fierce whisper to Lydia, "Who's bidding against me? Thought this would be a snip."

"I don't know," said Lydia. "But if you're not careful you'll be pushed right over your limit."

"By Saint Patrick and the Holy Spectrum," snorted the Professor, "there's no limit to a thing like this!"

Lydia smiled to herself at her father's passion.

"Some day," she said, "you must tell me what the Holy Spectrum is."

"One thousand five hundred," said a voice from the far back of the crowd. Swiftly though he screwed his head round to try and catch a glimpse of the other bidder, the Professor could not pick him out. Only Lydia at his side frowned sharply as she thought she now recognised the voice.

"Somebody else must have discovered it, too," groaned the Professor, then with a belligerent look at the auctioneer, he called, "Guineas!"

And the object of the rising emotion and frustration in the Professor's breast? Well, unless you happen to share his particular type of passion, you have little hope of understanding fully.

The Professor was a lover of old motor cars. He was a member of the Veteran Car Club and the Vintage Sports-Car Club. He already owned a 1906 Wolseley-Siddeley tourer, and still used a 1927 Alfa-Romeo 22/90 to drive himself about in. There is a distinction, of course, between Veteran, Edwardian, and Vintage in the motor-car world. Veteran cars must have been manufactured not later than 1904, then follows the Edwardian period from 1905 to 1916, and the Vintage cars run from 1919 to 1930.

The thing which the Professor thought that he alone had spotted in the list of contents for sale at the auction of an old country-house was a motor car. Under the heading *Miscellaneous* — immediately after *Outside Equipment and Garden Tools and Furniture* — it had been catalogued simply as *Sunbeam car, good running order*.

But when the Professor had come to view it before the sale he had realised with considerable excitement that this was the understatement of the year. The car was in fact a 1913 Sunbeam 12/16, a tourer, which to any lover of old motor cars was like an art dealer coming across an unknown Utrillo in an outhouse.

The auctioneer caught the Professor's eye as a voice from the back of the room said, "One thousand eight hundred pounds."

"Guineas!" the Professor fired back.

The auctioneer smiled happily. But there was no happiness in the Professor. To his increasing annoyance and frustration the unknown bidder outbid him all the way up to two thousand pounds. When the bidding reached that point even the Professor sadly recognised his limit, and the car was knocked down to the other man for that amount.

The Professor, fuming with disappointment and anger, stumped out of the room, got into his vintage Alfa-Romeo, and drove off, quite forgetting that his daughter, Lydia, had accompanied him to the sale.

Lydia did not mind this, however. She was used to her father's moods. She went out of the house, threading through the auction crowd, to the garage at the bottom of the drive. A young man was leaning against the door, eating a sandwich, a vacuum flask in one hand. He turned as she came up and grinned at her. He was a tallish young man of about twenty-five, blue-eyed, fair-haired, and his brown face was marked with a suspicion of freckles. His name was Richard Denby and he had met Lydia once before.

"Hi, there," he said pleasantly. "Cold day. Like a cup of coffee?"

Before Lydia could reply, he had filled a cup for her. He handed it to her with a little bow.

Lydia said, "We've met before, haven't we?"

"Lord," said Richard, "did I make such little impression? Yes, at the Hunt Ball two weeks ago. We had three dances together, and you only drank lemonade. As a matter of fact, I fell hopelessly in love with you. I still am, madly. Would you mind if I asked you to marry me?"

Lydia frowned. He was an attractive young man, and she remembered him well, but at the moment love and marriage were far from her mind.

"Why were you bidding for the Sunbeam?" she asked.

"This baby?" He nodded into the garage where the old car sat, its brass and bodywork sadly in need of polish. "Beauty, isn't she? Bit of work on her and you won't recognise her. Actually I wasn't bidding for her. Can't afford that kind of money. If I could, I'd be putting it into my business."

"Business?"

"You remember — I told you about it at the dance. I've just started a garage in Rivervale. Mean to have a string of them all over the country in the next ten years. No, in this, I was a kind of agent."

"Bidding for someone else?"

"Yes."

"Who?"

"Is it etiquette to say?"

"To hell with etiquette," said Lydia sharply. She could produce something of her father's directness when necessary.

"Just as you like," said Richard. "I'd break any rule for you. It was for Sir John Coddinstone. Told me to go up to three thousand if necessary."

"Sir John Coddinstone!" Lydia's eyes widened.

"Why'd you say it like that?"

A wry smile played about Lydia's lovely lips. "That's nothing to the way my father would say it if he knew. He and Sir John would cheerfully murder one another to get possession of, say, a Mercedes-Simplex."

"They're scarce."

"I know. There isn't much I don't know about cars."

"Excellent. You know, I've a theory that women should become car salesmen, I mean, saleswomen. After all, who decides on the family car, really? Why, the woman. You can have a job in my place, if you like —"

"You don't waste any time, do you? Which do I get first, the job or marriage?" Lydia smiled. "Anyway, you'd have to ask my father about marriage and when he knows about this —"

"You'll tell him?"

"Why not? You don't want things made easy for you, do you?"

"For you — no obstacle counts. Would you like a sandwich to go with that coffee?"

"No, thanks." Lydia put the cup down and walked away, but as she went she was smiling to herself. Of course, a girl would prefer to be wooed more romantically, but there was something refreshing about Richard Denby's directness, and she liked the way his fair hair strayed a little untidily over his forehead.

Actually Lydia did not have to tell her father about the way Sir John had outbid him at the auction. Sir John Coddinstone, C.B.E., J.P., head of Coddinstone Steel Products and a handful of other companies, now semi-retired, told the Professor himself. He arrived at the Professor's house, which was a few miles outside Rivervale, that evening at half past six in time to be given, reluctantly, a whisky and soda.

Between the Professor and Sir John there had existed, since the time they both went to the same public school together, a curious love-hate relationship. They were both quick-tempered men with wills of their own. At school they had competed fiercely for the last place in the cricket and rugby teams and for election to various exclusive societies. As young men they had fallen in love with the same girls and in retirement they had by chance settled in the same part of the country. The Professor, whose metallurgical researches had contributed to Sir John's business successes, had the pure scientist's indifference to wealth. He just regretted that his chosen field of research had brought him so much in contact with Sir John.

Life had never missed a chance to keep the feud going between them. It was typical of life that it had made them both keen Veteran car enthusiasts. Sir John owned and still used a 1928 Alvis 12/50, front-wheel drive, and could not have been more scathing of the merits of the Professor's Alfa-Romeo.

"Well, Fitzy!" bellowed Sir John, "I see you've done it again. Blast you!" Sir John was a large, jovial-faced, fleshy man, the same age as the Professor, and he habitually addressed everyone as though half a gale were blowing. His voice now made the glasses on the sideboard ring and the Professor wince.

"Done what? And don't shout at me. I'm not deaf, even if you are."

"I'm not deaf! And you know what I mean. I've just had a letter from the Secretary of Knight's saying I've been blackballed again. That's the fifth time."

Knight's Club, of which the Professor was not only a member, but also Chairman of the House Committee, was an exclusive London club, where one could eat well and in comfort, where the port was excellent, and the stakes at cards as high as one cared to make them. It had long been Sir John's ambition to become a member.

The Professor shrugged his shoulders. "Somebody there doesn't like you. Plain. Why keep on trying?"

"Somebody!" Sir John took a turn up the room, paused at the sideboard and helped himself to another whisky and soda. "It's you, Fitzy! Every time my name comes up you slip in the one black ball that counts against me. Damn rotten show. After all, you've got nothing against me really. I mean, not from a club point of view."

"No?" The Professor lit his pipe unhurriedly. Then he went on, "A club, Coddy, is a place where a man goes to relax, to be with friends, to enjoy himself. He doesn't want to meet people there he doesn't want to meet. Whole idea of a club. Now take you — ever since you turned up at school with me, I've been runnin' into you all over the place. Turn a damned corner, no matter where, and there you are. But not at Knight's. I can't tell you what a joy it is, Coddy, to be certain that every time I go through the door of Knight's I know that you can't follow."

"Dashed unfriendly. Just because I squeezed you out of the rugger team, and then that young girl —"

"Old history, Coddy. Go away, there's a good chap."

"I will. But I'll tell you something — I got the Secretary's letter this morning. If I'd been elected, I was going to let you alone to bid for that 1913 Sunbeam just out of gratitude. But not when I learnt you'd done it again. Yes — don't look so pop-eyed, Fitzy — it was me bidding against you, through a young feller called Denby who's just started a garage in Rivervale. Any time you care to withdraw your objection to me bein' a member of Knight's, Fitzy — then you can have the Sunbeam for two thousand pounds."

"Bribery — by all that's holy!" The Professor was on his feet.

"Prejudice!" Sir John smacked his empty whisky glass down. As they glared at each other, Lydia came into the room.

"What are you two shouting about?" she asked.

"Shouting?" Sir John looked amazed. "Just thanking your Father for the drink, my dear. Must be on my way, eh? Good night, all."

When Sir John had gone, the Professor poured himself a stiff drink, muttering to himself as he did so.

Lydia said, "There's a young man to see you."

"Send him away."

"I can't. He wants to ask you for permission to marry me."

The Professor spun round. "Marriage! Is this, the day of my greatest tribulation, the time to be introducing such a subject? It's more like murder, I feel!"

Lydia smiled. Before her father could say more she went to the door and opened it.

"Come in," she called.

Richard Denby entered the room.

"Daddy," said Lydia softly, her eyes on Richard, "this is Mr. Richard Denby, who wants —"

"What name?" the Professor roared.

The door closed as Lydia retired. Richard, wincing a little at the roar, stood his ground by the door.

"Denby, sir."

"Denby — the garage bloke?"

"Yes, sir."

Perhaps it would be as well to draw a veil over the rest of the very short and mostly one-sided conversation. A few minutes later, as Richard left the house, Lydia appeared from the bushes at the drive side and, chuckling, said, "Don't talk now." She slid into the spare seat of his car and went on, "Just drive to Rivervale. The Rose and Crown. You look quite pale and you need a drink."

"For a moment," said Richard faintly, "I thought I'd never get out of there without needing medical attention. I had no idea that a Professor knew such language!"

"They pick it up over the years from their students," said Lydia.

"You've no idea what he asked Saint Patrick to do to me — with the help of something called the Holy Spectrum."

"Drive, don't talk," said Lydia. "I'm thinking."

Richard didn't know it, and some men much older and more experienced than he would not have known it, but Lydia had just uttered the most dangerous words a woman can utter. *Don't talk, I'm thinking.* They always mean that a woman wants something and is determined to have it.

When Lydia returned home that evening, the Professor was waiting up for her. Lydia was late because the restorative drink she had offered to Richard had been reciprocated by an invitation to have dinner with him. She came in, humming gently to herself, her blue eyes sparkling.

The Professor greeted her without preliminaries. "Damned cheek of that young man, Denby."

"Oh, I don't know," Lydia said airily.

"Well, I do. Damn it — he bid against me for the Sunbeam on Coddy's behalf!"

"He's got nice manners and I like the way his hair goes."

"By all Ireland's green acres, girl! You don't marry a man for that kind of thing. Besides, you can't marry until you're twenty-one without my permission. And anyway, twenty-one or not, if you married a man who had caused so much sorrow to your old father, I'd turn you out —"

"Into the snow?"

"Depends on the time of year. And I'd cut you off without a shilling."

Lydia smiled. "You've been reading some old-fashioned novels, Daddy."

"They're the best. Anyway, what I mean is you wouldn't get my blessing."

Lydia nodded gravely. "That's different. I'd like your blessing. Why are you so prejudiced against him? You don't know him. It's just like you are with Sir John. He's a nice man but you persist in fighting each other, when you'd both like to be friends."

"Friends — with that awful money-grubber Coddy! Heaven Forbid! And I forbid you to see this young man."

"Sorry, Daddy, I can't refuse to see my employer."

"Employer!"

"Yes. He's given me a job as a car saleswoman. I start tomorrow morning. Could I interest you in a new car?"

"No, you couldn't!" barked the Professor. "There hasn't been a decent car made since 1930! The only car you can interest me in is that 1913 Sunbeam Coddy stole from me."

"Stole?"

"As good as."

"I heard him offering to let you have it for two thousand if you'd support his application for Knight's."

"By the Holy Spectrum — you think I'd do that! Bandy a club membership about for money! Coddy must be losing his grip to imagine such a thing. Sacrilege!"

For a moment Lydia was silent, thinking. Then she said softly, "No two women would behave as stupidly as you two men. Something must be done about it … Yes" — there was a faraway look in her eyes — "something must be done."

"I don't know what you're talking about, girl. Go to bed. And you're not to take that job, and you're not to encourage that young Denby."

Lydia came over, kissed the top of his head, and then went off to bed.

The next morning she was at the Denby Garage ready for work at nine o'clock. That the labour relations between employee and employer were going to be amicable was established by the fact that her new boss greeted her in the office with a kiss which Lydia showed no signs of not enjoying.

Nevertheless, as they parted, she said, "One thing I will not do is marry without Daddy's blessing. At the moment, as far as you are concerned, Richard, I might as well enter a nunnery. We must think of something to make him change his mind."

"Of course," said Richard, his eyes on her full of love and admiration, knowing that he had never seen nor ever would see anyone half as lovely. "You do that."

This last sentence proved Richard to be a young man of good sense. He knew that changing men's minds was woman's work.

A week later, on a Monday morning, Professor Patrick Walter Fitzharris received in the post a typewritten letter from Sir John Coddinstone which read as follows:

Dear Fitzy,

It was unpardonable of me, of course, to offer to sell you my 1913 Sunbeam in return for your support to my next application for membership of Knight's. I can only put down my lapse of good taste to stress of emotion. However, since I know the strong sporting instincts and the love of a wager which distinguishes all members of Knight's, I am prepared to issue the following challenge. I will race you over a thirty-mile course on Wivenhoe

Beach, cars to be used — my 1913 Sunbeam against your 1906 Wolseley-Siddeley. Stakes — if you win, you take the Sunbeam, and if I win, you support my application to Knight's.

Yours,
Coddy

Surprisingly enough, Sir John Coddinstone also that morning received a letter from the Professor. It read:

Dear Coddy,

I've been thinking about this club affair. The offer you made about Knight's and the Sunbeam was in pretty bad taste, even for you. But underneath I suppose you're not a bad old scout. Tell you what I'll do, I'll give you a sporting chance. I'll wager that in my Wolseley-Siddeley tourer I can beat you in your Sunbeam over a thirty-mile circuit on Wivenhoe Beach. Stakes — if you win, I'll support your application to Knight's, and if I win, I take the 1913 Sunbeam.

Give me a ring before I change my mind.

Yours,
Fitzy

Within five minutes Sir John was on the telephone to the Professor.

"Well, Coddy?"

"Well, Fitzy?"

"My Sunbeam will leave your scrapheap miles behind."

"I doubt," said the Professor icily, "whether you'll even get that box of chair springs of yours to start. If you do, it'll break up with metal fatigue after a mile."

"I will meet you at Wivenhoe Beach this afternoon at two-thirty to agree a course."

"Do that."

At lunchtime that day the Professor told Lydia — who showed no surprise at the news — about the challenge, and finished, "I'll have to spend some time tuning up the engine, getting everything in racing trim. I wondered if you'd care to give me a hand — that is, if you can spare time from that, job of yours which I forbade you to take."

"I shall be glad to help, Daddy. And thank you for inquiring about the job. Yes, I'm doing very well there and I'm very happy in my work."

"You're as devious as your mother was at times," said the Professor. "And almost as good-looking." He smiled at her.

Meanwhile, at Sir John's house the same lunchtime, young Richard Denby was getting his briefing.

"I don't care what you've got on hand at your garage, my boy. Drop everything and get cracking on that Sunbeam. I want it in tiptop condition by next Monday for this race. Spare no expense. If I win, I might put up a little money for your next garage. Might, I said — it depends."

Later that afternoon, the Professor and Sir John met at the beach. Wivenhoe was a five-mile stretch of isolated sand, ideally formed to be the jousting place of these hard-bitten knights of the wheel. The two of them walked the bone-hard sand together, a stiff early spring breeze battering them. They agreed on a course four miles long with a post at each end for turning markers, and they settled for four complete laps.

From the top of the cliffs, Richard and Lydia watched the two men below. Richard, his arm round Lydia, said, "I still don't understand. Only one of them can be the winner.

Either the Professor gets the Sunbeam or Sir John gets into the club. How does that help us?"

"You want to marry me, don't you?"

"Of course I do!"

"And you know I won't without my father's blessing. When the parson says, 'If any man can show just cause' — you know the bit — he's capable of jumping up and starting an argument."

"But I still don't understand how this race helps us."

"You will. Now listen and concentrate. What I want from you are two simple mathematical calculations."

Richard listened, his eyes widening, his admiration for Lydia increasing …

So, for the next few days Richard and Sir John worked on the Sunbeam, tuning it up and grooming it into tiptop racing trim. Elsewhere, the Professor and Lydia did the same for the Wolseley-Siddeley.

Oddly enough, when the day of the race came, Lydia, pleading a headache, said she could not go to the race. She felt more like going to bed. She got the Wolseley-Siddeley out of the garage for her father, and he set off for the drive to the beach by himself. The moment he was gone, Lydia's migraine disappeared and she went off to the Denby Garage in Rivervale in the highest of good spirits.

When the Professor arrived at Wivenhoe, Sir John was already there, and with him was Richard Denby.

"Brought Denby along as starter. That all right by you, Fitzy?"

The Professor grunted.

The two cars were lined up alongside the starting post. The long stretch of sands ran smoothly towards the distant cliffs, and far out could be glimpsed the creaming breakers of the sea. A few seabirds wheeled round, crying, and a thin spring sun shone bleakly down. The cars, hoods down for racing, looked magnificent. The Wolseley-Siddeley, its green-and-red bodywork sparkling, was a little higher and older fashioned in line than the Sunbeam, whose cream-and-chocolate body gleamed as though it were glowing with some inner health. Brasswork dazzling the, eye, they made a magnificent pair.

The Professor pulled on an old motoring cap, donned goggles, and said, "Well, let's get started, and remember, Coddy — the chap who's ahead has the right to cut in. If you don't give way — then by Saint Patrick that's your funeral."

Sir John pulled on a woollen balaclava hat and goggles and said, "I'm not going to be behind at all, so there's no question of me giving way. Denby will count down from ten and then give us the starting gun."

Richard watched the two men climb into their cars. The engine notes increased a little and they sounded solid, throaty, ready to go.

He began to count. "Ten, nine, eight, seven …" And as he did so, he hoped fervently that he had worked out correctly the little calculations Lydia had given him. If he'd made a mistake he knew there would be hell to pay from Lydia.

"Three, two, one —"

He fired the starting gun and the engine growls rose to a crescendo and the cars were away, their back wheels spinning for a moment on the hard sand.

It was a race which Richard was to remember with pleasure all his life. He, too, was a lover of old cars and here, on this lonely beach, to see this road-hardened pair, one from 1906 and the other from 1913, still full of power and fight, spurt away down the hard yellow sands, was an inspiring sight. They roared away from him, engines and gears whining as the drivers made their changes, their bodyworks flashing red and green, cream and chocolate, the stiff spring wind taking their exhaust fumes, and the sun sparkling on their brasswork. It was a wonderful moment.

Richard walked up the steeply sloping beach to a sandy bluff and pulled out his fieldglasses, training them on the cars.

A quarter of a mile from the start Richard saw that Sir John in the Sunbeam had drawn just ahead of the Professor in the Wolseley-Siddeley and, when he had a clear lead, he pulled over, dead in front of the Professor. At the post marking the turn for the first half-lap, Sir John hugged the corner too tight and went wide as he came round into the straight. The Professor, obviously doing some very quick gear changing, pulled sharply inside him and went ahead by about a length.

The two cars came roaring back up the course and Richard saw that the Sunbeam was again drawing ahead. But Sir John could not get enough lead this time to head the Professor and, with a hungry roar of engines, back wheels flinging up great sprays of sand, they took the turn at the end of the first lap abreast. A mile down the straight of the second lap, Sir John went into the lead and increased it by the time he came to the post. This time he cornered more carefully, holding his ground, and he came roaring up the back end of the lap with the Professor a good hundred yards behind him.

At the end of the third lap, Sir John had a lead of three hundred yards. As the Professor took the turning-post behind him, Richard saw him thumping at the steering-wheel with one hand as though he were a jockey whipping up his mount to greater speed.

Sir John went into the first half of the last lap well ahead. He took the far turn, his lead increasing, and came charging into the home stretch, the sun gleaming on the Sunbeam's brass and paintwork. Behind him came the Professor, bare-headed now for the wind had swept away his cap.

Then, a mile from home, it happened. Richard saw the Sunbeam suddenly lose speed and then slowly come to a halt. Sir John leapt out and raised the engine cover. As he did so, the Professor, his exultant shout carrying on the wind, one hand raised derisively at Sir John, swept by in the Wolseley-Siddeley. But a hundred yards beyond the Sunbeam the Wolseley-Siddeley, too, suddenly lost speed and finally came to a halt. The Professor leapt out, too, and his head was soon stuck into the engine.

Richard walked down towards them. By the time he reached them, both gentlemen had discovered their trouble and Sir John had joined the Professor.

"By the Holy Spectrum!" cried the Professor. "We've both run out of petrol. No race."

"We'll run it again tomorrow." said Sir John.

"Without petrol," said Richard, "you're both in trouble right now."

"Why?" demanded the Professor.

"Because," said Richard, "it'll be high tide in another hour." He nodded out across the sands where the breakers of the fast incoming tide had grown larger. "And even between the three of us we can't push these machines up the steep sand slope from the beach."

"But we must get the cars off the beach!" roared Sir John. "If the tide gets them, they'll be ruined. You're a garage man, get up to the coastguard station and phone your place for a towing vehicle. It can be here in twenty minutes."

Richard went up to the coastguard station and on his way he was congratulating himself on his mathematics. While Lydia and he had been working on their respective cars, they had drilled holes in the petrol tanks nicely and mathematically calculated in diameter, to ensure that there should be a wastage of petrol from the time they unplugged the holes when the cars started for the beach.

Half an hour later, with the tide now coming dangerously close, Lydia arrived, driving a towing vehicle from the garage. She roared down to the beach and drew up by Sir John and her father. She jumped down, a slim, smiling girl, the sky-blue overalls, with Denby's Garage in bright red letters across the front, matching the blue of her eyes.

"Get our cars out of here quickly!" cried her father.

Lydia shook her head and tossed the ignition keys of the towing vehicle in her hand. "Not so fast, Daddy. At Denby's we always like to settle the charge for rescue work before we begin."

"Damn the money, Lydia," snorted Sir John. "We'll pay what you ask."

"I know you will. But the job can't be done for cash. Now let's see …" Lydia frowned and rubbed a hand thoughtfully across the fair brow.

"Hurry, Lydia," growled her father. "The tide's coming in fast."

Lydia pulled a sheet of paper from her pocket.

"You'll both have to sign the contract. Here's a pen. I'll read the terms for you. 'In return for salvaging the two cars the following is agreed. One, Professor Patrick Walter Fitzharris agrees to support Sir John Coddinstone in his application for membership of Knight's. And, two, the aforesaid Sir John agrees to sell his Sunbeam to the aforesaid Professor for two thousand pounds.'"

"Blackmail," protested the Professor.

"Extortion!" roared Sir John.

"Goodbye," said Lydia, and began to move towards her vehicle.

Both men shouted together, "Agreed!"

Lydia came back, smiling, and this time she had her arm linked in Richard's. "Also," she said, "the aforesaid Professor agrees to give his permission and unqualified blessing to the marriage of Lydia Annette Fitzharris to Richard Cromwell Sylvester Denby."

"Is this a moment to waste time in idle talk of marriage?" cried the Professor.

"Give me that pen," said Sir John. He took the pen and the contract and signed it. Then he handed them to the Professor.

"Fitzy, old fish," he said, his grey eyes twinkling, "one way and another we've both been done — and by an absolute charmer. Better sign and look happy. Seem to remember that your wife's father didn't think much of you to begin with. But you turned out fairly all right. So will young Denby. How can he go wrong with a girl like Lydia to manage him? Sign."

The Professor raised the pen over the contract, looked from Richard to Lydia, and then, his blue eyes sparkling, grinned.

"Why not? But by Saint Patrick, there's going to be a court of inquiry about this petrol business. Something fishy there."

"Later," said Lydia, as he signed. "Just now we've got work to do. Come on, Richard, let's get these old crocks off the beach."

"Old crocks!" The voices of the Professor and Sir John were raised in a unanimous roar of indignation that drowned for a moment the noise of the breaking surf.

The Ballerina and the Pigs

When the question of sending Assistant Commissar Pyotr Danilov to England to buy pigs was discussed there was a difference of opinion. "He is too young. The English farmers would cheat him," said the President.

"He is twenty-eight and with a youthful countenance, I admit," said the Minister of Agriculture. "But he knows pigs, and his father was a peasant. He will make no bad bargains."

"English farmers have a drink called cider which is drunk the whole time a bargain is being made," said the Minister of Propaganda and Culture. "It would confuse his judgment."

"You forget we have a drink called vodka," said the Minister of Agriculture dryly. "Young Pyotr can drink even Commissar Androv, my deputy, under the table."

"Well ..." The President hesitated. "In the last two years we have had five assistant commissars go West on such missions and they have never come back. It looks bad." He glanced across at the Head of the Secret Police. "What do you think?"

The Head of the Secret Police, who had been leafing through a decadent democratic magazine full of photographs of bathing beauties — lent him by the Minister of Propaganda and Culture — said finally: "Pyotr is a firm believer in our way of life and would never desert it. Moreover, he has a good head for drink and bargains. Let him go. Also, there is a delicate little matter which needs attention in England. He will make no trouble about it. Send him."

So Pyotr Danilov was sent to England. He spent a month in Somerset making purchases for his government. At the end of that month quite a few farmers respected his capacity for cider and his eye for a pig. And quite a few farmers' daughters tried to make him stay in England, for with his fair hair and blue eyes, a charming smile, and a well-built muscular body, Pyotr was a man to attract a girl's attention. They were wasting their time.

One farmer who, rashly egged on by his daughter, offered Pyotr a partnership if he wished to stay, regretted it. Pyotr sat up all night with him, drank him out of cider, and when the dawn came was still demonstrating how good life was behind the Iron Curtain..

"Oi tell 'e," said the farmer afterwards, "Oi damned nearly went back with 'e. That there convincin' 'e was. Charm a bird off a tree, 'e could."

Two days before Pyotr was due to fly back with his consignment of pigs, a man joined him at the bar of the Castle Hotel in Taunton. He was a short, dark-looking man with a permanent twitch to his upper lip and an astonishing capacity for whisky acquired after two years' service in the London embassy of Pyotr's country. Pyotr knew him well for he was the commercial attaché who had arranged all his contacts and finances on this trip.

The man called for a whisky and when it came lifted the glass and said: "Bung ho!"

Pyotr frowned. He disapproved of the acquisition of foreign habits. "Is everything arranged for the flight back?" he asked.

"No hitch. One of our own planes comes in tomorrow and you go off the next day. Pigs for the People's Democracy. I've never flown with pigs. What do you do to keep 'em happy? Sing to them?"

"If they show any signs of restlessness," said Pyotr stiffly, "I inject sedatives."

"Needn't do it with this lot. Just unpack Nadia Mariac and get her to dance for them."

"I do not understand," said Pyotr, and he stroked the beginnings of a fair moustache which he was growing to give his face more sternness. Nadia Mariac had been a member of the State Ballet, but a year before she had defected from the company while on a European tour and had taken asylum in London.

"She'll be with you. In a packing case marked 'Antibiotics.' Drugged, of course. Our police boys picked her up four days ago at Brighton. Did you get to Brighton? Typical Western decadence ... I go there most weekends."

"You mean," said Pyotr offended, "that I am to take her back? And you tell me this in a public drinking place?"

"Where'd you want me to tell you? In church? All business is done in bars over here. You must know that."

"But this is a secret service matter. I'm here for pigs."

"Don't worry. The airport people will give no trouble. Just tip her out of the case when you're airborne and then hand her over when you touch down. It ought to be a hell of a trip. Snow storms all over Europe is the forecast."

He gazed into the distance over his glass. "Nadia Mariac ... What a lucky man you are! Now, I wouldn't mind going home if I had her company on the way."

"That is no way to talk, comrade," said Pyotr crossly.

"I wasn't talking. I was ruminating. She's a wonderful creature; like a naiad, like the dream of all the world. She's going to find it hard work in the salt mines. Still, I suppose she must be shown the error of her ways."

"She must. And many others, too," said Pyotr curtly. But as he left the bar he was thinking that they ought not to have done it. Each department, in a well-run state, should look after its own affairs. Pigs and ballet dancers didn't mix.

There were fifty pedigree pigs, mostly young sows and boars, and one enormous sow due to farrow in a few days. For this last Pyotr had developed an extraordinary affection and respect. He had bought her from a best-selling author who ran a pig farm for tax evasion purposes, and she was a champion. From her loins, thought Pyotr, would spring a race of pigs that would enrich the impoverished strain of his own country.

Lady Chatterley was her pedigree name. "Give her love," the author-owner had said, "she thrives on it. It breaks my heart to part with her, but for good red gold I would sell my mother."

"She shall have every attention," said Pyotr, who had fallen in love with her on the spot. She was the size of a walrus, but not so good-looking, and with an endearing habit of charging her pen wall down and going berserk if not fed on time.

During the first fifteen minutes of being airborne Pyotr had his hands full of the pigs, and particularly of Lady Chatterley. They all showed signs of being annoyed at this unusual procedure.

Pyotr walked up and down between the crates and stalls that had been fitted into the fuselage, and he talked to his charges in a calming, comforting voice. Gradually the restlessness disappeared from them.

Carl and Ugo, the two pilots who had come over with the plane, glanced back and watched this performance with amusement. Between them was a large earthenware jar of cider, a parting present from the embassy's commercial attaché and, unknown to them, laced with whisky. Lacing cider with whisky is like putting a match to gunpowder, only rather slower in effect.

"Sing to them," called Carl.

"Let Nadia out," added Ugo. "She will dance for them."

"Your duty is to pilot and navigate this machine," said Pyotr coming up the catwalk to them. "Attend to it! The woman will not be released until we are well over the sea. We might yet have to make an emergency landing."

"He thinks of everything," said Ugo.

"I remember Nadia in Swan Lake," said Carl. "Like thistledown. I have had her picture over my bed ever since."

"With twenty others," said Ugo. He reached for the cider jug, but Carl beat him to it.

Pyotr went back to Lady Chatterley. She lay on her side and sneered at him. He gave her an apple and she ate it, blowing long sighs through her nose. Above her, through the fuselage window, he could see the piled winter clouds, and far below, the grey edge of the sea tilting over the shrinking lip of the land.

Half an hour later he went to the tail of the plane where a large wooden case was stored. It was stamped all over: EXPORT ONLY. ANTIBIOTICS. KEEP AWAY FROM DAMP.

Ugo came up behind him and handed him a hammer and a chisel. "We're well over the sea."

Pyotr began to work on the case. He got the top off and between them they tipped the crate on to its side. Beautifully packed, Nadia Mariac came out like a Christmas present, untouched, unblemished, fresh and lovely, and sleeping peacefully.

"It'll be half an hour before she comes round," said Ugo.

"And in a filthy mood," called Carl.

Pyotr scarcely heard them. He was looking down at the figure of Nadia Mariac. Ugo had slipped a couple of rugs under her and she lay with one cheek resting on her hand. She was beautiful, with the longest lashes and the shapeliest legs Pyotr had ever seen. What a pity that so beautiful and talented a creature should have been politically so misguided! She had done his country a lot of harm when she had deserted the State Ballet. It was good, Pyotr thought, that now the Minister of Propaganda and Culture would be able to announce that she had returned of her own free will, disgusted with the western world.

He reached down and pulled her rumpled skirt lower over one of the loveliest knees he had ever seen.

An hour after take-off they were running into very bad weather.

"If it gets any worse," said Carl to Pyotr, "maybe we should land at Vienna."

"We go straight through," said Pyotr. "The sooner I get the pigs back the better."

"And Nadia?" asked Ugo.

"The pigs are my chief concern," said Pyotr stiffly. "We need them to improve our blood strain. Basically, we are an agricultural country. Our industry is growing — but to give it strength it must be supported by agriculture. In these pigs lie the health and vitality we need for the future. Why the police should go to all this trouble to get back this misguided ballet dancer, I can't think. She has been corrupted by the West. Like all artists, she is unstable and a liability, incapable of appreciating the glorious future which awaits us if we all dedicate ourselves to the simple, human truths of pure socialism."

"Oh, shut up! " said a voice.

The three men looked round. Nadia Mariac had come up behind them. Tall, dark and slim, she was frowning at them.

Ugo smiled. "Mademoiselle," he said, "I have long been an admirer of yours. I trust you slept well, and I assure you that, for my part, you could have stayed for ever free — I mean, in the West."

"Me, too," said Carl.

"I strongly disapprove of such talk!" snapped Pyotr, and he stroked his incipient moustache and looked stern.

"I'm sure you do," said Nadia. "I've met your kind before. You've swallowed the bait, the hook and a good length of line. That pig speech of yours was just too pompous, and you've no idea how silly you look when you try to be stern." She nodded at the jug which Carl was raising. "What's that?"

"Cider, mademoiselle."

Nadia took the jug and drank deeply.

"It is advisable to be careful with that," said Pyotr. "It is very strong."

"It's what I needed. A drink and a cigarette."

"Allow me." Ugo was on his feet with his case out.

"Certainly not," said Pyotr. "The smoke will upset my pigs. I cannot think why people find it necessary to drug themselves with tobacco."

"The People's Democracy finds drugs very useful at times," said Nadia.

"You will oblige me, mademoiselle," said Pyotr, "by keeping to the rear part of this machine and not talking with the pilots."

She looked at him for a moment, then turned and went back to her crate.

An hour later and the weather was worse. They were flying in cloud, fighting a headwind and swift showers of sleet and snow.

Carl said, "We ought to come down at Vienna to refuel."

Pyotr said, "You have plenty of petrol."

Ugo said, "But bucking this headwind will use it up. We ought to refuel. Besides, Vienna is a beautiful city."

"Very beautiful," said Nadia from her seat on the packing case. "I have danced there twice. We could take the Commissar Danilov to some night clubs."

"Assistant Commissar! And we do not come down at Vienna," said Pyotr. "That is an order. Do not imagine that I am unaware of your hopes. It would be easy for you to escape there."

"Would it matter?" asked Nadia. "Why don't we all escape? I have very good friends in Europe who would give Carl and Ugo jobs, and you, Assistant Commissar Danilov … well, we could set you up in a pig farm."

"A good idea," said Carl, swaying in his seat gently.

" Excellent," said Ugo, putting out a hand to steady him.

"This conversation shall be reported to the appropriate authorities," snapped Pyotr. "Meanwhile, we go on." To emphasize his words he pulled a revolver from his pocket.

"He's incorruptible," said Carl.

"Adamant," said Ugo.

"Pig-headed," said Nadia.

Much later, they were really in trouble. The weather was still bad. Darkness was not far off and, according to Ugo, they were only a short distance from the mountainous frontier of their own country. The petrol was very low. In addition the port engine was giving trouble.

Carl said, "I shall have to look for a place to land."

"Keep on," said Pyotr. "This is a trick."

"Not this time," said Ugo, nodding at the fuel gauge. "Those headwinds have taken it out of us. And listen to that engine."

"Good! Maybe we shall crash," said Nadia. "It is better to die than to go to the salt mines."

"We shan't crash," said Carl hazily. "I am a good pilot and full of good spirits. But I suggest that you all go up into the tail, just in case."

"Keep on," said Pyotr stoutly, waving his revolver.

"Don't be an ass," said Nadia. "If you shoot him we shall crash anyway. Also, when we come down it will be in our own country, so you have nothing to fear."

"It is my pigs I think of. A crash might bring on a premature delivery for Lady Chatterley."

"It is a risk that pig mothers must face if they start flying," said Ugo, and he stood up and led Pyotr towards, the tail. "Carl, you had better SOS our position," he said.

They did crash. Not badly, but enough. Carl brought the machine down through the clouds into a landscape of snow-covered peaks, grey and indigo with the first night shadows. He picked a long valley running down from a high main ridge. He had only enough petrol left for about five minutes' flying, and the faltering port engine made things worse.

But the greatest handicap was the cider laced with whisky which he had taken. There was a long open stretch of snow running down between a fringe of dark pine woods. The trees seemed to dance all over the place.

Back in the tail Ugo cried, "Hold tight!" and he put his arm tightly round Nadia's waist to steady her. Pyotr clutched the side of Lady Chatterley's stall and talked soothingly to her.

They hit the ground, softly at first, bouncing on the smooth snow, and then there was a great splintering crash. Pyotr was jerked forward and his head hit the corner of the packing case. Darkness closed on him like an iron curtain …

When Pyotr came to, he was lying in a large four-poster bed. Sunlight came streaming through a low window which gave him a glimpse of wooden houses and the snowy slopes of a hill dotted with dark pine trees.

Standing at his bedside was a man of about sixty, bluff and brown-faced, and with a thatch of long white hair. He extended an arm and patted Pyotr on the cheek. He wore a leather waistcoat, blue trousers and a yellow shirt, and he had the appearance of an amiable brigand — which in many ways was exactly what Jari Demaru was.

"Welcome, Assistant Commissar Danilov," he boomed. "The whole village welcomes you. We pray to the Holy Mary and her angels and out of the sky she sends help … Wonderful!"

"What" — said Pyotr a little weakly and realizing that his head was bandaged and aching — "happened?"

Nadia Mariac moved into view. She was dressed in a red skirt, her hair tied back with a ribbon and her arms bare from a loose blouse.

"We crashed. That was yesterday. But Carl managed to send an SOS giving our position first. This is Jan — he keeps this inn."

"And Lady Chatterley?"

"Doing fine!" roared Jan. "A litter of eight, all of them sturdy."

Pyotr began to struggle up. He must go to her at once. But Jan pressed him back. "Don't worry. Tomorrow you can get up, but you're still weak. When you've had some food and wine you'll be better. Until then —"

"But the other pigs," said Pyotr.

"They are being looked after," said Nadia; and she glanced at Jan a little awkwardly.

It was at this moment that Pyotr became aware of a most fragrant odour seeping into the room through the open doorway. Suddenly, as though he had received an electric shock, he jerked upright in bed.

"I can smell roast pork!"

"Of course," Jan soothed him. "Didn't I say you were our saviour? For two months we have been snowed up. This summer our crops failed and our cattle died of a disease. The whole village was starving. The authorities have done nothing about sending us relief. So, we thought —"

"You mean, you've killed one of my pigs!" shouted Pyotr.

"Two," said Nadia. "There are thirty people in the village. One would not be enough."

Pyotr leaped out of bed and then jumped back again. The nightshirt he had been given was absurdly short. He began to shout and storm. The pigs were for breeding purposes. They were not to be eaten. He forbade it …

It was the beginning of a long argument that carried through intermittently to the next day, when he was well enough to get up and go down to the main room of the inn. There, confronted by Jan and the village elders and Carl, Ugo and Nadia, he had to face facts. There was no food in the village. The people had to eat.

"Which is better, to save the lives of thirty people, or to suffer a little loss to your breeding stock?" asked Jan.

"But the authorities should have sent you food," said Pyotr.

"We are snowed in. It is difficult. Personally, I think they wish us to leave the village and this is their way of doing it."

"Why should they wish you to leave?"

"Because … Well, we are near the frontier and occasionally we do a little smuggling. You must yourself have enjoyed a contraband cigar —"

"I don't smoke."

"Then a glass of whisky, or given your girl friend a pair of American nylons —"

"I have no girl friend. And no more pigs are to be killed. The authorities have heard our SOS. They will soon dig their way into the valley and bring help."

"Let us hope so," said Jan.

"The pigs are valuable," declared Pyotr. "Help will come, without doubt."

"Maybe," said Nadia. "It is a pity the authorities have not come before this — with food for the villagers. But then they are not pigs."

Pyotr glowered at her. But underneath he was a little disturbed. The authorities should have done something.

He went out to see the pigs and Lady Chatterley. They were all housed in a barn at the back of the inn. Lady Chatterley lay on her side looking very pleased with herself. It was a fine litter.

As he stood there Nadia came up behind him. "They look sweet," she said, leaning over and picking up one of the litter.

"Please," said Pyotr. He took the piglet from her and restored it. "They can easily be injured by improper handling at this stage."

"You are very fond of animals?" asked Nadia.

"It is my work."

"You take it very seriously."

"Life is a very serious business. We have the future to think about."

She was looking at him curiously. "You don't smoke. You don't have a girl friend. You have only the future. You are very good-looking and strong. I think you are kind, too. Will you really let them take me away with the pigs and put me in a salt mine?"

"It is nothing to do with me."

"You know what will happen to me in a salt mine?"

"Please ..."

"You do not like to think of it." She came closer to him. "You find me beautiful?"

"Yes."

"You do not want to kiss me, like Carl and Ugo? Perhaps then you would change your mind about handing me over. You could say I escaped when the plane crashed."

Pyotr frowned. "You are wasting your time."

Nadia smiled. "How can you tell until you have had the kiss?" Suddenly her arms were around his neck and her soft, warm lips on his. After a while Nadia stepped back. "You will change your mind?"

"No," said Pyotr. But he couldn't get any sternness into his face, and his voice was weaker.

Behind them Lady Chatterley suddenly rose and charged her pen bad-temperedly. It was time for her feed.

Two weeks went by and no rescue party came. Pyotr began to feel desperate. As he couldn't stand by and see people starve, ten of his pigs had been eaten. And almost as bad as the pig situation was the Nadia situation. Jan and his villagers were quite prepared to smuggle her over the frontier. But not if Pyotr was going to inform against them.

Nadia herself was still trying to make Pyotr change his mind. Three or four times a day he would turn a corner and find himself in her arms or, as he bent over Lady Chatterley's pen, suddenly feel Nadia's soft lips on the back of his neck.

It was wearing him down. In bed he dreamed about her. Lying awake in the dark he could hear her voice. "You're too nice to give me up. I like you, I really do. Underneath that Party manner you're human. Why don't you escape with me?"

It was a constant barrage. And when she was in his arms, or her lips were on his, it was hard for him to remain resolved in his principles.

Late in the afternoon of the fifteenth day rescue came. A lorry fitted with caterpillar tracks was seen coming up the valley. The whole village assembled outside the inn to welcome it.

Five minutes later Pyotr was closeted with Commissar Androv — his superior at the Ministry of Agriculture — in Jan's little sitting room.

Commissar Androv was a big-jowled, dark shaven man with eyes like Lady Chatterley. He was in a bad temper, too.

"But why have you been so long?" asked Pyotr.

"Because the SOS position was given wrongly. Your pilot is a fool. We've been looking in the wrong valley. And then it took four days to cut through into this one. What about the pigs?"

"They're safe, but —"

Pyotr told him of the villagers' plight. And he finished, "But now you've come with food, they will be all right."

Commissar Androv rose and his face was working with anger. "You're a fool, Danilov! I've brought no food for them. They're a thorn in our side with their independent ways. And if you've let them have the pigs to eat you've not only countenanced the destruction of valuable government property — but you've also interfered with the policy of population redistribution."

"But you can't let people starve."

"In a planned economy, and if policy dictates it, you can," shouted Androv.

Pyotr's lips tightened and his face now had a sternness which no one could ignore. "People are more important than pigs."

"That's treason! You've bungled your mission. Assistant Commissar Danilov, you are under arrest … And personally I think you'll either be shot or sent to forced labour. And now, where is the girl Nadia Mariac?"

Pyotr stood up. Almost before he knew he was saying it, he heard himself shout: "Arrest me if you like. I've done no wrong. But you can't have her. She escaped back over the frontier following the crash."

"Further bungling! You'll be shot all right …"

"Go to hell!" snapped Pyotr, and his eyes were blazing.

Pyotr was left in the room. Commissar Androv went out to superintend the loading of the pigs on to the lorry. He was hardly out of the room before Jan entered.

"I was listening," he said. "What are you going to do?"

"Face a trial and rely on the justice of the People's Democracy."

Jan rolled his eyes. "You like to learn the hard way. You'll be shot. Nadia's hiding in the woods. As soon as it's dark she's going over the frontier with Ugo and Carl. You could join them."

"Never! This is my country."

An armed guard came into the room. "Out!" he said to Jan. "This man is under arrest."

From the window, which overlooked the village square, Pyotr watched the lorry being loaded with pigs. The sun was dropping behind the mountains and the pines were throwing long shadows across the snow. Three soldiers, Jan and some villagers — under Commissar Androv's direction — were helping with the loading.

They couldn't shoot him, Pyotr told himself as he watched. He'd done no wrong … But could he be sure? The government would have let the villagers starve. Policy … Maybe it would be policy to shoot him.

He saw Lady Chatterley's litter being carried to the lorry, and then came Lady Chatterley, swaying along. They took some time getting her up the ramp into the lorry, but eventually it was done. The guard, watching with Pyotr, said: "All right. Let's go."

Pyotr was marched out of the inn, the guard behind him with his rifle at the ready.

Commissar Androv carne up to him.

"You get up in the cab with me and the lorry driver," Commissar Androv ordered.

As Pyotr moved to the front of the lorry his eye caught Jan's. Jan was standing at the side of the lorry fastening a rope. Maybe it was something in Pyotr's face, or maybe it was just because Jan was so much older and wiser than Pyotr. Anyway, as Pyotr passed, Jan reached inside the lorry and jabbed a long needle into Lady Chatterley's fat flank.

The effect was tremendous.

There was a great, grunting roar of pain from Lady Chatterley. She charged the side of the flimsy stall that had been rigged up at the end of the lorry and crashed through it. Ploughing into the other pigs she carried them before her like a bow wave. The mass of animals thundered against the tailboard of the lorry. The fastenings broke and an avalanche of pigs cascaded to the ground.

A moment later Lady Chatterley and the other pigs were charging across the village square.

The guards and villagers behind the lorry went down before the rush. Commissar Androv leaped round, swearing and shouting to Pyotr's guard to get after the pigs. For two or three moments a squealing, grunting confusion existed in the square while panicking pigs dashed in all directions.

Jan dropped quickly to Pyotr's side. "Run, you fool!" he hissed. "Nadia and the others are up by the crashed plane. I'll see that no one chases you."

Pyotr didn't move.

Run, fool!" urged Jan. "Don't you want to see Nadia again? To be kissed by her? To feel her arms around you? Run!"

Pyotr began to run. Commissar Androv saw him. "Get him!" he bellowed at Jan. "Take some villagers and get him."

"Yes, commissar," said Jan. "But I should point out that if you want to round up these pigs, they were now all heading for the woods down the valley with the guards and villagers after them — you'll need all my people's help."

"Get that man first!" Androv pointed to the small figure of Pyotr racing across the snow towards the head of the valley.

"Yes, commissar. But it may take hours. When darkness comes soon any pig not caught will freeze to death. Pigs are valuable. The country needs them. A man could be shot if he went back to the capital without them, pleading that he thought it better to let them freeze while he went after a traitor. Pigs, not people, are what you have to consider."

Commissar Androv's face gradually inflated. Then he burst out, "Damn you! Pigs then, first."

He and Jan began to lumber down the valley which was noisy with the shouts of the guards and the villagers and the high, frenzied squealing of pigs.

Pyotr went racing across the snow and into the pine trees where the plane had crashed. Nadia, with Ugo, Carl and two guides from the village who were to take them over the frontier, was waiting there.

"You left it almost too late," said Ugo.

"Forward to freedom! " said Carl. But Nadia said nothing. She didn't have to. She just looked at Pyotr and smiled, and Pyotr suddenly put his arms around her and kissed her.

"Break it up," said Ugo.

"Time for that later," said Carl. And they started walking.

Preview

Young Paul Ashcroft has travelled to the beautiful French Riviera. His goal: to make a lot of money. His methods: more than questionable.

Following his motto 'the world owes me a living', he steals and swindles – using what he needs for himself and passing on the rest to those less fortunate.

But just as Paul's schemes and tricks begin to be fruitful and he falls in love with the intriguing Elise Benoit, someone appears to be onto him...

Young Man on a Bicycle, by Victor Canning

Also Available

Mr Edgar Finchley, unmarried clerk, aged 45, is told to take a holiday for the first time in his life. He decides to go to the seaside. But Fate has other plans in store…

From his abduction by a cheerful crook, to his smuggling escapade off the south coast, the timid but plucky Mr Finchley is plunged into a series of the most astonishing and extraordinary adventures.

His rural adventure takes him gradually westward through the English countryside and back, via a smuggling yacht, to London.

Mr Finchley, Book 1

OUT NOW

About the early works of Victor Canning

Victor Canning had a runaway success with his first book, *Mr Finchley Discovers his England*, published in 1934, and lost no time in writing more. Up to the start of the Second World War he wrote seven such life-affirming novels.

Following the war, Canning went on to write over fifty more novels along with an abundance of short stories, plays and TV and radio scripts, gaining sophistication and later a darker note – but perhaps losing the exuberance that is the hallmark of his early work.

Early novels and story collections by Victor Canning –

Mr Finchley Discovers His England

Mr Finchley Goes to Paris

Mr Finchley Takes the Road

Polycarp's Progress

Fly Away Paul

Matthew Silverman

Fountain Inn

The Minerva Club

The Aberdyll Onion

Young Man on a Bicycle

About the Author

Victor Canning was a prolific writer throughout his career, which began young: he had sold several short stories by the age of nineteen and his first novel, *Mr Finchley Discovers His England* (1934) was published when he was twenty-three. It proved to be a runaway bestseller. Canning also wrote for children: his trilogy The Runaways was adapted for US children's television. Canning's later thrillers were darker and more complex than his earlier work and received further critical acclaim.

Note from the Publisher

Printed in Great Britain
by Amazon

60599343R00116